Fuel for the fire

A crash from behind Kenyon made him gasp. He threw up his hands, expecting the remainder of the roof to crush him. Instead, he turned to discover that the wall behind him was dropping away brick by brick.

Kenyon leaned through the opening. The tunnel beyond was lit with a faint gray glow from some unseen source. He saw a stream of sluggish water and damp moldy walls. The smell was unbelievably rancid. But compared to the fallen hallway, it looked like paradise.

The ceiling overhead groaned again. Kenyon scrambled through the hole and splashed into the sewage tunnel seconds before the rest of the roof would have fallen on him.

He stared at the rubble-filled hole he'd just exited. "Harley," he whispered. He did not expect a reply, and he did not get one. He knew he would never hear her voice again. She couldn't possibly have escaped the destruction of the underground lair.

Harley Davisidaro was dead.

Don't miss any books in this thrilling new series:

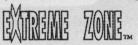
EXTREME ZONE™

Available from ARCHWAY Paperbacks

EXTREME ZONE™

INHUMAN FURY

M.C. SUMNER

AN ARCHWAY PAPERBACK
Published by POCKET BOOKS
New York London Toronto Sydney Tokyo Singapore

This book is a work of fiction. Names, characters, places, and
incidents are either products of the author's imagination or
are used fictitiously. Any resemblance to actual events or locales
or persons, living or dead, is entirely coincidental.

AN ARCHWAY PAPERBACK *Original*

 An Archway Paperback published by
POCKET BOOKS, a division of Simon & Schuster Inc.
1230 Avenue of the Americas, New York, NY 10020

Produced by Daniel Weiss Associates, Inc., New York

ISBN: 0-671-01412-9

First Archway Paperback printing October 1997

10 9 8 7 6 5 4 3 2 1

AN ARCHWAY PAPERBACK and colophon are
registered trademarks of Simon & Schuster Inc.

EXTREME ZONE and the EXTREME ZONE logo are
trademarks of Daniel Weiss Associates, Inc.

Printed in the U.S.A.

IL 7+

For all the people on the BBS,
who keep me on my toes.

P R O L O G U E

The jaguar slunk between the trees. Cloud-softened moonlight shined down around it, filtering through the leaves and dappling the animal's glossy black fur with patches of silver and gray. The broad, padded feet of the great cat stepped with a hushed whisper that barely disturbed the debris of the forest ground. The smooth muscles of its shoulders bunched like bands of steel beneath the black velvet of its coat. With infinite grace, the cat strolled across a moonlit clearing toward a tight cluster of alder trees.

The passage of the jaguar sent a screech owl hurrying up from among the weeds. The bird's wide wings chopped at the air as it sought distance from the paws of the cat. The jaguar turned its green eyes toward the bird and made a soft rumbling growl, but it wasn't really interested. Tonight, it was on other duty.

There was a light ahead. Through the screen of alders a pale blue glow cast long shadows across the clearing. The jaguar paused, its extraordinarily light sensitive eyes adjusting to the illumination. Then it trotted ahead, slipped between two smooth trunks, and entered the tight circle of alder trees.

In the center of the alder circle was a low table, a computer, and a woman. She sat cross-legged in the

1

green grass, leaning toward a computer screen that was crisscrossed by lines of text and the shadowy outlines of some broken design. Her bare limbs gleamed like marble in the glow of the screen.

The woman inclined her head as the jaguar drew near. "Restless, Riassa?" she asked. "Already tired of the hunt?"

The big cat paused beside the woman and rumbled softly.

"I feed you too well," said the woman. "That's the problem. You're losing your edge." But as she chastised the jaguar, her left hand reached out and found the soft fur of the cat's throat. Her fingers rubbed along its flesh, kneading the loose skin and soft, short coat.

With her other hand, the woman took hold of the mouse attached to the computer and pushed it a few inches forward. As she did, the image on the screen expanded. The strange design was revealed as tight clusters of road, streets, and alleys, each of them labeled in sharp glowing letters. As the display continued to grow, a point of red began blinking in the grid.

The woman took her hand from the computer mouse and stared at the circle of flashing pixels. Her lips pressed together into a hard, bitter line, and she slowly shook her head. "This is a bad business, Riassa. Very bad. But *oh*, how fascinating it can be."

The jaguar answered with another soft rumble.

The big cat looked up at her, pale light from the computer screen reflecting in its eyes.

With unconscious grace, the woman unfolded her legs and rose to her feet. She stepped quickly through the surrounding circle of alders and passed along the forest trail. Her bare feet moved along the packed earth as silently as the padded paws of the jaguar at her side.

The path the two companions followed twisted beside a small pool, then turned up and over a knob of lichen-stained granite. The sharp, clean smell of cedar filled the air as the hardwood trees became mixed with tall, straight conifers. Wildflowers clustered in the shadowed corners of the wood, lending sparks of pale lavender petals and white blossoms that seemed to glow.

Then, abruptly, the forest ended.

It didn't end at the edge of a glade, or even at the shore of some shadowed river. It ended at a wall of cool, gray-gold glass.

The woman pressed her hand to the glass. Beyond, the view dropped away for forty stories. Far below, a million sparks of light outlined the city blocks, while streaks of headlamps showed traffic moving slowly along the roads.

Mixed with the ordinary traffic was the pulsing red glow from police cars, ambulances, and fire engines. Even through the glass, the woman could hear the thin high sound of sirens as the horde of vehicles gradually drew together. At the center of this gathering was a small building almost hidden by taller structures on either side. From the small building, a twisting column of smoke was rising up to dissipate in the dark night sky.

The jaguar grumbled.

"Yes," the woman said with a nod. "It's almost over now. We are reaching the grand finale."

Ten blocks away, the base of the column of smoke turned into an explosion of flame. An orange fireball boiled up from the small building, and for a moment the city was lit as brightly as noon.

The woman smiled. The jaguar growled again, its voice dropping to a note so low, it was almost beyond hearing.

"Don't worry, Riassa," said the woman. She took her hand from her head and stroked the fur at the big cat's neck. "It's all going according to plan." The woman returned to the window and looked at out at the red flames and the rising clouds of oily smoke.

"I think events in this city are about to become interesting, Riassa," she said softly. "Very interesting. And if Harley Davisidaro should have once again managed to survive, well . . . we'll remedy that, won't we, girl?"

The big cat rumbled in agreement.

4

Kenyon Moor's skull felt packed with broken glass.

Twists of rusty barbed wire seemed to run along his nerves. His blood pulsed in his veins with searing pain as though it had been replaced by a mixture of acid and liquid fire. His arms and legs felt as if they had been beaten with iron bars, and an entire crew of miners seemed to be digging into his forehead with pickaxes.

Behind the lids of Kenyon's tightly closed eyes, images whirled and danced like a movie gone mad. He strained to remember where he was. For a moment, Kenyon had a vision of a brightly lit room, a gleaming steel table. He felt a flush of fear as he remembered a doctor leaning over him. But the man hadn't really been a doctor. He'd meant to hurt Kenyon. A tall blond woman also had been nearby, a woman with sharp, savage features. Someone else had been lurking in the corner—another man?

And Harley. She had been there. Kenyon had to get back to Harley.

He felt a fresh surge of anxiety. He strained to get up. He had to help Harley. Kenyon had one clear image of Harley Davisidaro's heart-shaped face looking down at him, her dark eyes wide with concern.

5

Then rational thought was torn away by a fresh wave of agony.

For an unknown length of time, Kenyon swam in a sea of madness and pain. A tangle of distorted images rolled through his mind, set against a background of fire and smoke. Hot and cold chased themselves across his skin. Odors and tastes plagued him in an insane tumble of sensations.

Gradually, the memories of the past days surfaced out of the chaos and pain. Kenyon remembered how Agent Ian Cain had appeared in Stone Harbor, terribly wounded and begging for Harley's help in fighting a threat to his mysterious organization. Cain had also needed a fresh transfusion of the strange liquid he used as blood. From the beginning, Kenyon had been against helping Cain. To him, Cain was only another of the secret people— the people who pulled the strings of the world without anyone's knowledge or permission. Kenyon only had agreed to help Cain because Harley had insisted. Together, Kenyon and Harley had followed a string of clues to St. Louis, where they had found an underground lair waiting under the dusty rooms of an old bookstore.

His memories of their journey became tinged with black wooziness as Kenyon recalled their encounter with Mr. Antolin, the immense blob of a man who controlled the strange underworld. He remembered the torture room, and the fire, and a vast, world-ending explosion, but darkness was flowing into Kenyon's mind like some warm, heavy fluid. The memories of Antolin and his gang of killers began to become swallowed up by drowsy unconsciousness. Kenyon felt a surge of fear that bordered on panic, but even that quickly washed away as the warm darkness gathered. He felt a great gulf opening, ready to drag him down into its endless depths.

Open your eyes, ordered a voice that cut through the darkness. The voice seemed to issue from inside Kenyon's aching head, but somehow it didn't seem to be coming from any part of his own mind. *Get up,* the voice demanded. *Now. She needs you.*

Whatever the source, the voice was insistent. Kenyon fought off the desire to slip into the thick, comfortable blackness that promised to let him forget his pain. With an effort that felt like lifting a thousand pounds, he opened his eyes.

At first, what he saw with his eyes open didn't seem to make any more sense than the chaos that had swarmed behind his closed eyelids. Streamers of smoke passed in front of him, obscuring his vision. When the smoke cleared, a series of dull red rectangles slid by above him. Then he was plunged into darkness. Then it was light again, the rectangles shifting overhead.

After a moment, he realized that he was moving. It took several seconds to figure out that he was facing the brick ceiling of a subterranean tunnel, and a few more seconds to discover that he was being dragged along a hard stone floor that was littered with chunks of broken stone and charred wood.

Kenyon raised his pounding head from the floor and strained to focus on his feet. Bloodstained hands were wrapped around his ankles. The hands were attached to the muscular arms and heavy shoulders of a short, stocky man. The man was shuffling backward down the hallway, dragging Kenyon as he went, with the rubber soles of his shoes squeaking along the floor.

The man was a mess. Lank gray hair dropped away from a scalp that was matted with dark red blood. More blood stained the man's blue surgical clothing, and a sluggish stream of crimson ran down into the thick hair on his arms. From the gray pallor of the man's skin, Kenyon didn't think he had a lot of blood to spare.

Only the torn and bloody clothing allowed Kenyon to recognize the man—it was Caska, Antolin's chief torturer. The torturer had been dressed as a doctor when Kenyon had first seen him. He had been neat, clean, and meticulous as he uncovered his tools of pain. But now as he labored down the hallway, Caska no longer looked like any kind of doctor. In addition to the cuts on his forehead and arms, Caska's lips were split and swollen. As he opened his mouth to breathe, Kenyon saw the jagged stump of broken teeth. The torturer looked exactly like what he was—an ugly, sweating brute.

A jab of pain shot through Kenyon as he was dragged over a sharp-edged piece of rubble. Without thinking, he moaned and raised his injured shoulder from the ground.

At once, Caska's impossibly deep blue eyes widened. "You're awake," he gasped.

Kenyon licked at his dried lips and gave the man a grim smile. "Brilliant observation," he groaned. He wrenched his legs out of Caska's hands, drew a deep breath, and kicked out at the torturer with all the force he could muster.

Caska grunted in surprise and pain. He stumbled backward.

Shards of agony sliced through Kenyon's skull. He rolled onto his elbows and started to climb shakily to his feet. Since his parents' death, he had spent months training to fight with and without weapons. He knew a hundred ways to knock the stocky fake doctor to the ground and a dozen methods of killing him bare-handed. But none of the training Kenyon had undergone had prepared him to fight when his head was full of fire and his stomach was rolling with nausea. He rose as far as his knees before a wave of dizziness crashed over him and drove him back to the cold stone floor.

"You must come with me," said Caska. With his broken teeth and bloody lips, the man's voice was thick and blubbery, like a man talking under water. A fine spray of blood came out along with his words. "Mr. Antolin is waiting."

Kenyon knew why Mr. Antolin needed him. The owner of this subterranean lair was fat. More than fat. *Huge.* In comparison to Mr. Antolin, the largest Sumo wrestler would have been a scrawny supermodel. The man was so obscenely massive that he wasn't able to move an inch from the couch where he'd lain when Kenyon and Harley had been introduced to him.

Before Mr. Antolin had sent Kenyon off to be tortured, the fat man had claimed to have a device that would free him from his grotesque bulk—by moving his mind into Kenyon's body. The whole idea seemed completely ridiculous. Kenyon had seen some strange things since he began his private war with the secret organizations, and Harley had told of things that were stranger still. But the idea of a machine that could transfer someone's mind from one body to another was too bizarre to consider. Still, Kenyon had no intention of letting Mr. Antolin put his idea to the test.

Caska staggered toward Kenyon and clamped a bloody hand on his shoulder. "You must come with me," Caska repeated. "Mr. Antolin needs you."

Kenyon stretched out his hand and found a length of broken wood on the floor. It was jagged at both ends, fire-blackened, and too short to be a proper club, but it was the best weapon available. He gripped the splintery wood tight in his right hand, rolled left, and slashed at the torturer.

The sharp point of the wood tore through the

sleeve of Caska's surgical scrubs and opened a fresh wound in his already bloody arm. The fake doctor gave a high-pitched scream and drew back.

Kenyon gasped in pain as he tried again to get on his feet. The room swayed around him, and he had to brace his free hand against the curving wall of the corridor, but he managed to stand.

"You . . . you must come," Caska repeated a third time. The expression on the torturer's face said very clearly that this was *not* how the world was supposed to be. He was supposed to hurt others, but Kenyon didn't think this man ever had expected to be hurt himself.

"Forget it," replied Kenyon. He raised his makeshift club. "Show me where to find Harley, and *maybe* I'll let you live."

Caska blinked his dark blue eyes in confusion. "But—," he began.

From somewhere behind him, Kenyon heard a dull thump. A rush of hot air swept past him, and the floor of the tunnel swayed like a ship on stormy seas. His trembling legs buckled and he slumped to his knees as dark smoke rolled through the corridor, bricks cracked and fell away from the ceiling, and streams of plaster poured down like loose sand.

"You—I—we have to go," Caska stammered. The torturer had stayed on his feet during the explosion, but he looked weaker and more confused than ever. "Mr. Antolin is—"

In the distance, Kenyon heard another heavy

thump of an explosion, followed by a sharp, whistling sound that grew swiftly louder in the dim corridor. A moment later a flash of ripping pain lanced through Kenyon's left shoulder. He gasped, dropped his club, and reached toward the source of the agony. His hand found warm flowing blood and a shard of twisted metal jutting from the muscle near his shoulder blade.

"We must—," Caska started, but he was interrupted by the whistling sound. This time it was louder.

Kenyon flung himself against the hard stone of the dirty, debris-strewn floor. He raised his face an inch from the ground and looked up.

Caska only stood there, looking weak and bewildered.

The whistling sound rose to a banshee wail. Kenyon felt another bolt of pain as a metal fragment buried itself in the meat of his thigh. Compared to what happened to Caska, it was less than a scratch.

A flight of metal shrapnel shrieked over Kenyon like a squadron of terrible birds. The torturer was struck by small fragments in his chest, his arms, and his face. Then a chunk of metal the size of a baseball broke through the ribs on the right side of the man's chest with a noise like branches snapping. Before the torturer could fall, a sharp-edged fragment as big as an ax blade chopped into the side of his skull. With a soft, gurgling cry, Caska slumped to the ground.

Kenyon lay there for several seconds, staring at the dead man as blood pooled among the debris on the floor. When the whistling sound did not come again, Kenyon finally dared to press his hands under him and lift his body from the rough floor. With every movement, pain screamed from the metal fragments embedded in his shoulder and leg. Kenyon twisted around and reached down to the dull piece of iron that jutted from his thigh. Biting his lip, Kenyon grabbed the bloodstained metal and gave a sharp tug. It slid from his leg with a soft, sickening noise, leaving behind a rip in his pants leg and a slowly widening circle of blood.

Kenyon reached back over his shoulder and tried to pull out the other bit of shrapnel. It was in an awkward position. He could just manage to graze the metal sliver with the fingers of his right hand, but each touch only drove the jagged shard further into the muscles of his back. Kenyon took a deep breath and held it as he stretched his arm around as far as he could. His fingers brushed the fragment once, twice, and then he got a grasp on its rough edges. Even then, the metal resisted. Kenyon's breath escaped between his lips in a shout of pain and a red haze spread over his vision as he tore the fragment loose and flung it to the floor.

For at least a minute, he sat motionless in the dark tunnel. Between the pain of his wounds and the continuing ache in his head and limbs, Kenyon wanted nothing more than to lie down and sleep for a week. Or maybe a month. Only the waves of smoky heat were rolling through the corridor and the sound of further explosions in the distance told him this was no place for a nap.

Still, Kenyon might have stayed and rested for a little while if it wasn't for the thought of Harley. Harley was somewhere in this underground madhouse, and he was the only one who could rescue her.

Kenyon peered through the blue-white fog of smoke and plaster dust that obscured the hallway. He hoped to spot something familiar, but this hallway didn't look like any part of the path that Kenyon and Harley had followed into this labyrinth. There was no sign of the room where Kenyon had been taken to be tortured—and no sign of Harley.

He spotted the length of broken wood he had used as a weapon lying on the floor of the passage. He picked it up, stood, and began to limp down the corridor, in the opposite direction that Caska had been dragging him—toward the source of the explosions.

"Harley!" he shouted into the smoke. "Harley! Are you there?" Somewhere in the distance, Kenyon heard something fall, and a gust of hot, smoky air whipped past his face, but he received no reply to his call.

Kenyon's leg ached at every step, his head swam, and blood ran down his back, but he staggered on down the dimly lit hall. Harley might be anywhere in the smoky passages. The thought of her lying some-where ahead—injured, burned, maybe even dying—drove Kenyon to limp forward ever faster.

In all the time he had known Kathleen "Harley" Davisidaro, he had never admitted how he felt about her. In his own mind, he had listed reason after reason why he shouldn't get involved with her. Harley had her own problems and her own set of strong opinions. Whenever Kenyon talked to her, they argued more often than not. Besides, Harley obviously had feelings for the missing Noah Templer.

Any rational person could see that there was no way Kenyon and Harley would ever have more than a friendship. Kenyon knew all the reasons well enough, but the facts didn't make a bit of difference to how he felt. Harley was the most complex, the most *complete* person that Kenyon had ever met. She was strong, re-sourceful, even ruthless when she had to be. But she was also caring, thoughtful, and fiercely loyal to her friends. The death of Kenyon's parents had left him feeling nothing but rage and a desire to destroy everyone who had hurt him. But all of Harley's per-sonal tragedies—while just as terrible as his own—had not killed her hope.

And that was why Kenyon loved her.

He paused as he reached a pile of rubble and then picked his way carefully around a spot where the ceil-ing had partially collapsed. A length of copper pipe hung down through the shattered roof of the tunnel, and for a moment Kenyon was cooled by splashing water. But he had scrambled no more than a dozen yards past the busted pipe before he began to hear the sounds of fire crackling and hissing in the corridor ahead.

The smoke in the hallway grew thicker, and Kenyon was forced to crouch down to find breathable air. He saw a light in the distance. Some of it was the orange light of flames, but he also could make out the white glow of electric lamps. He crept on for another hundred feet, turned a corner, and found himself facing a new passage.

To his right, the hallway ran through dancing tongues of flame and extended into darkness. The left fork of the corridor was more brightly lit, and less than a hundred feet away Kenyon saw the doorway leading into the torture chamber. But the hallway in between the place where he stood and the entrance to the room was choked with walls of roaring yellow fire. The door to the torture chamber might as well have been on the far side of the moon.

"Harley!" Kenyon shouted again.

He heard a noise. It sounded like people shouting. Or maybe fighting.

Kenyon stepped closer. The fire burned along the walls and sent rippling sheets of smoky orange flames spreading across the ceiling. Its heat was so great that Kenyon almost expected his own skin to cook.

"Are you there, Harley?" he shouted.

Hot wind sucked the air from his lungs as he strained to hear a reply. It was hard to make out anything above the roaring fire, but this time, Kenyon thought he heard someone calling to him. He couldn't make out any words, but he was almost certain he heard Harley's voice somewhere ahead.

"Hang on!" cried Kenyon. Still grasping the rough wooden club, he put his arms in front of his face, drew in a deep breath, and prepared to dash through the inferno.

A hand landed on Kenyon's shoulder.

His heart jumped in his chest, and he spun around, expecting to see the ruined, bloody face of the torturer. What he saw was worse.

One of the people who had led Kenyon into the torture chamber had been a tall man in a black hood. Now that man was in front of him again—only he wasn't a man at all.

The hood had been torn open in a dozen places. The figure's clothing was also shredded. It hung in ribbons from his arms and draped over his chest in tatters. Through all the gaps in the man's clothing, Kenyon could see . . . nothing. With the fire burning so close, there certainly should have been enough light to see the man's features. Instead, the torn hood was filled with midnight darkness. Everywhere the clothing didn't cover, the man was absolutely flat black, without any highlight or reflection.

Kenyon had never seen such a thing before, but Harley had told him about encountering similar creatures. "A shadow man," he whispered.

In reply, the dark figure delivered a sharp, back-handed slap that knocked Kenyon against the wall. He gasped in pain as his wounded shoulder was smashed against stone. For a moment, he was too stunned to move. Then he remembered the club in his hand.

Kenyon raised the rough piece of wood, and drew back his arm. As the shadow man stepped toward him, he drove the sharp end of the wood straight into the creature's chest.

The wood splintered as if he had tried to drive it through a sheet of steel, and a painful reverberation shot up Kenyon's arm. The shadow man knocked the remaining stump of a club from Kenyon's hands with a blow that left his fingers numb.

Kenyon ducked another swing of the creature's hand, dodged left, and drove his fist into the shadow man's gut.

Then he screamed.

The thing's flesh was so hard that Kenyon was sure his hand had broken. And it was cold—excruciatingly cold. Though he touched the shadow man's dark substance for no more than second, a thin glaze of frost now covered Kenyon's hand and arm.

The shadow man grabbed Kenyon by both shoulders, lifted him from the ground, and flung him down the hallway away from the torture chamber. Kenyon's lungs seared with hot air as he passed above licking tongues of fire. He landed painfully on the other side of the flames in a place where the floor was covered in a jumble of broken stone and fallen, charred timbers.

Kenyon had just enough time to sit up and watch as the shadow man stepped into the fire. He hoped that the flames would destroy the creature. Instead the fire turned blue and retreated from the dark thing's path. The creature closed on Kenyon, its hands stretched out to hold him in a freezing grip.

Kenyon looked at the debris around him. It was only rubble. There were no weapons to be found. Moving on all fours, he scrambled away over the broken stones. The floor under his hands was hot, and the air was so smoky he could hardly breath. With his eyes watering and his breath burning in his throat, Kenyon struggled to his feet and staggered into the darkness with his hands held out in front of him.

For twenty feet, he stumbled over fallen wood and shattered stone. He hoped there might be another opening ahead. If he could escape the shadow man, he might still circle back and reach Harley. Then his fingers touched hot, cracked brick.

Despair swept over Kenyon as his hands swept left and right. He couldn't feel an opening. It was a dead end.

He turned around to see the shadow man slowly approaching. "Where?" it asked. Its voice was deep and held no trace of any human emotion.

Despite his fear of the creature, Kenyon blinked, confused. "What?"

"Where is he?" the shadow man demanded.

"He?" Kenyon frowned. "Who are you talking about?"

Before the shadow man could reply, the roof overhead groaned like a giant breathing out his last immense breath. Both Kenyon and the shadow man glanced up as the roof of the tunnel split open and dark earth came plunging down.

The collapse of the tunnel seemed to go on for hours, although it couldn't have lasted more than a few seconds. Bricks fell, along with chunks of concrete, asphalt, and old granite paving stones from some long-buried street. Electric wires pulled free in showers of blue sparks.

Kenyon pressed himself flat against the brick wall at the end of the passage and turned his face from the tumbling stones and streaming earth. He had been educated at a fine private school, and Dante's *Inferno* had been required reading. As the stones roared down, the fire crackled, and smoke clouded the air, he felt like one of the characters in Dante's novel—cast into the lowest reaches of damnation.

The shadow man raised its dark arms and deflected the first stones that fell on top of it, but the creature was standing directly underneath the collapse. In a matter of moments, it was battered to the ground. Further along the passage, the ceiling gave way in one place after another, until the whole world seemed caught up in a great crashing wave of stone.

Then, almost as quickly as it had begun, the collapse was over.

In the aftermath came total darkness and an eerie silence. Kenyon coughed the dust out of his lungs as he reached out cautiously. No more than two feet from where he stood, the corridor ended in a barricade of debris. His slight touch was rewarded with a rumble and a stream of soft, sloughing mud sliding over his hand.

Kenyon turned around in a slow circle, exploring his dark prison with his fingertips. The roof might not have fallen on him, but the collapse had left him trapped in a space no more than three feet wide. He was buried under the earth. Soon enough, the roof would finish falling, or he would simply run out of air. Already the small space felt stuffy.

A knot of hysterical laughter rose into Kenyon's throat, but he choked it off before it could escape his mouth. He was alive. All he had to do was think.

A crash from behind Kenyon made him gasp. He threw up his hands, expecting the remainder of the roof to crush him. Instead, he turned to discover that the wall behind him was dropping away brick by brick. The masonry hadn't been able to withstand the pressure of the roof's collapse.

Kenyon leaned through the opening. The tunnel beyond was lit with a faint gray glow from some unseen source. In that infinitely dim light, he saw a stream of sluggish water and damp moldy walls. The smell was unbelievably rancid. It was not the most inviting place Kenyon had ever seen, but compared to the fallen hallway, it looked like paradise.

As if to speed up his decision, the ceiling overhead groaned again. Kenyon managed to scramble through the hole and splash into the sewage tunnel less than a second before the rest of the roof would have fallen on him.

He paused there in the dim gray light and stared at the rubble-filled hole he'd just exited.

"Harley," he whispered. He did not expect a reply, and he did not get one. He knew he would never hear her voice again. She couldn't possibly have escaped the complete destruction of Mr. Antolin's underground lair.

Harley Davisidaro was dead.

TWO

Harley Davisidaro stood at the edge of the sidewalk and watched the flames rise from the devastated bookstore into the night sky.

"Miss?" asked a voice at her side.

Harley ignored the voice. *Kenyon is dead,* she thought, aching with despairing sadness. That same thought had been running through her mind ever since she had escaped from Mr. Antolin's underground hideaway. The phrase was like a tune that had gotten stuck in her thoughts and wouldn't let go—the most awful tune imaginable.

A fireman in a yellow slicker and matching helmet stepped in front of Harley and peered at her through a plastic face shield. "Miss, are you all right?" he asked.

Harley heard the man's words, but the question made no sense to her. Of course she wasn't all right. How could anyone be all right after experiencing the horror she'd just managed to survive? All she could think about was Kenyon strapped to the torturer's table and the flames rising up to fill the hallways and rooms of the underground chamber. Harley had faced down Mr. Antolin and the assassin called Till, but she had not seen what happened to Mr. Antolin's other helpers or to Kenyon. It didn't matter. She didn't have

23

to see. There was no way anyone could have lived through the incredible furnace of fire and smoke that had razed Mr. Antolin's headquarters.

Kenyon is dead.

"Come on, Miss. You need to move back." The fireman reached out a gloved hand, took hold of Harley's upper arm, and began to pull her back from the fire. For a moment, she resisted, then she gave in and let the fireman lead across the sidewalk into the broad street beyond.

"You stay here," the fireman instructed her gently. "All right?"

Harley nodded. "All right," she replied in a weak, distracted voice.

The fireman stared at her through his plastic face shield for a moment longer. Finally, he turned away and hurried to help the others who were battling the blaze.

Harley stared off into space. She couldn't believe how much had happened so quickly. Only two days before, she had been back in Stone Harbor, sitting on the beach and wondering if anything interesting was ever going to happen again. Things had definitely gotten interesting.

First, assassins had trailed her to Stone Harbor and tried to kill her. Before Harley could recover from that shock, the mysterious agent who called himself Ian Cain had arrived in town. Cain had been wounded, and apparently dying. He told a complex story about his own unnamed secret organization and how they were being shattered by betrayal and greed for power. A splinter group within his organization was seeking to kill the remaining agents and seize all the power for themselves. If Cain had been telling the truth, the whole world was in danger from these renegade agents who were trying to take over his group.

Harley had been both frightened and determined. Cain had helped her in the past, and she had wanted to return the favor. She set out to find the strange artificial blood that could save Cain's life, find out what was going on in his organization, and put a stop to the threat of the splinter group. It had all ended in disaster.

A sharp stab of guilt hit her as she remembered arguing with Kenyon. He had wanted to stay out of it and let the groups argue among themselves. Harley had argued that they had to get involved. She wished bitterly that she had lost that argument.

She'd even lost the vial of greenish fluid she'd worked so hard to protect as she'd escaped the lair. Without a transfusion of the strange blood, Cain would certainly die. Harley had been sure she'd seen the vial still unbroken moments after she'd staggered out of the burning basement, but after that she'd somehow lost it in the confusion of being pulled to safety by the firefighters.

Harley was momentarily shaken from her dark thoughts as another pair of pumper trucks arrived in a flurry of sirens. More firefighters hopped down from the trucks and began to drag their gear toward the flames. Soon the street was crisscrossed by heavy hoses that pulsed and heaved. Pairs of firemen wrestled with the ends of the hoses and directed thick arcs of water into the rising inferno.

Harley could have told them it was hopeless. The bookstore that had covered Mr. Antolin's hideout was a tall, exotic structure, studded with cupolas, gargoyles, and granite. And it was filled, from basement to rafters, with thousands upon thousands of books and magazines. Some of the books were rare first editions that might have been sold for megabucks at an auction. Others were shoddy paperbacks that had already gone to rot and mildew. Now all of them were fuel.

By the time the first fire trucks had arrived, the fire had already reached the book stacks. The old yellowed paper had blazed as though it had been dipped in kerosene.

The windows on the ground floor of the bookstore exploded outward in a shower of glass that reached almost to Harley's feet. Blue fire jetted from the openings with a jet-engine roar, and she watched curling pages of magazines escape upward amid clouds of smoke and ash. The front doors bulged and split open like rotten fruit, dripping fire onto the sidewalk.

Harley watched it all as if it were something from a bad dream. She barely saw the firefighters that hurried past her. Even the flames, smoke, and crumbling structure of the bookstore made little impact on her mind. She was busy obsessing over the thought that she was doomed to lose everything and everyone that ever meant anything in her life.

Her mother had disappeared when Harley was small. Her father had been kidnapped by the military group called Unit 17. When Harley had allowed herself to get close to Noah Templer, he had been taken by the mystical Umbra. Then, just when it seemed as if Harley might get back both her father and Noah, the two of them had been lost into the unknowable depths of the white sphere. And finally, there had been Kenyon.

In some ways, Kenyon's loss was the worst of them all. Harley knew that Noah was, in some indefinable way, still alive within the depths of the white sphere. She could even communicate with him occasionally through brief, frustrating dreams. Harley's father might still be alive in the sphere, too. There was even a chance that her long lost mother still survived in some secret medical facility run by Unit 17.

But Kenyon was dead and gone.

What made the situation even worse was that Harley didn't even know how she felt about Kenyon. He and Harley had been arguing from the moment they had met. Kenyon had been so angry about the death of his parents, it often seemed that he couldn't think of anything but how to hurt Unit 17 and the other secret organizations. The idea that his out-of-control fury also hurt the people who cared about him hadn't seemed to occur to Kenyon. Any ten-minute conversation with him had been likely to leave Harley shouting and feeling ready to hit him with the heaviest object she could lay her hands on.

But on rare occasions, Kenyon had shown a gentler side. He had done things that were surprisingly nice and thoughtful—like paying for the beach house where Harley had been living without even telling her. According to Harley's friend Dee Janes, Kenyon had deep feelings for Harley that he had been afraid to reveal.

Harley supposed she had some feelings for him, as well. He was *attractive*. That is, if you liked the brooding, darkly handsome, worth-about-a-hundred million-dollars kind of guy. But Harley had Noah to think about. She had just started getting involved with Noah before he'd disappeared. She wasn't sure that she was ready to try again.

Not that it made any difference. Kenyon is dead, Harley reminded herself. She raised a dirty hand and wiped away fresh tears. She wouldn't have a chance to learn if their relationship would ever go further. There would be no chance for anything.

A sharp cracking sound from the burning bookstore caught Harley's attention. She looked up in time to see a section of the roof collapse inward, revealing a caldron of fire. Enormous tongues of flame reached up eagerly through the new opening. Taller buildings stood on either side of the bookstore, but the column of smoke and flame stood taller still.

The impossible situation didn't seem to discourage the firefighters. They sprayed their water through the shattered windows and sent it curving through the gap in the roof. White steam mingled with the black smoke of burning paper. Harley sat down on the rear bumper of one of the fire trucks and watched the hopeless fight.

Within an hour, a considerable crowd of spectators had gathered. More trucks rolled up to the scene, and policemen began to place barricades between the growing crowd and the fire. A policewoman approached Harley and asked her to move, but the fireman she had spoken to earlier hurried over. The two had a short, quiet conversation. After that, the police left Harley alone.

Harley supposed she should have left. After her father's disappearance, Unit 17 had erased all of Harley's governmental records and replaced them with information that made her look like a wanted criminal. To protect her, Cain had provided Harley with a new, safe identity. Even so, she had not gotten over her fear that some police officer would discover Unit 17's bogus criminal record, realize that her new set of identification was fake, and shut Harley away for a thousand years.

Sitting beside the burning bookstore, she found it hard to care whether or not she was arrested. Even if she ran away, she couldn't think of anywhere to go. The only people left in the world that even cared if Harley still existed were Dee Janes and Scott Handleson—and they were a hundreds of miles away in Stone Harbor.

Thinking of their names reminded Harley that Scott and Dee would probably be worried about her—with good reason. Harley had lost the airplane tickets she needed to get back, but she could go to a phone and call them. She dismissed the thought almost as soon as it occured to her. If she called Scott and Dee, the she would have to tell them . . . *Kenyon is dead.*

Through the cold hours of the night, Harley sat on the bumper of the fire truck and watched as the Washington Street Book Emporium burned. At some point during the night someone draped a jacket across her shoulders. Later, she found herself drinking from a thermos of coffee. But Harley couldn't remember how she'd gotten either of those things. Her anguish over Kenyon's death mingled with pure exhaustion to make the hours before dawn nothing but a long gray blur.

Finally, as the sky started to brighten in the east and a cold drizzle began dropping from the dark sky overhead, the walls of the old bookstore collapsed. Blackened stone gargoyles broke free from the corners of the building and came tumbling down to smash into dust on the sidewalk. For a moment, the whole store seemed to ripple in the heat, and then the walls tore open like sheets of paper. Showers of brick and plaster tumbled inward. Gradually, the whole building settled and slumped, falling into the pit left behind by the collapse of Mr. Antolin's underground chambers.

As the fire died, the firefighters moved closer. They directed their streams of water on the charred remains of the bookstore. A few even put on heavy, hooded suits and began to climb over the still-smoking heap of rubble.

"Excuse me."

Harley glanced up and saw a tall African American man staring down at her. He was a handsome, distinguised-looking man, with a square jaw, a nicely tailored suit, and a fedora perched on his head that reminded her of the one worn by Cain. Harley had never seen the man before in her life, but she would have bet a hundred dollars that he was some kind of cop.

"What do you want?" she replied. On a good day, she would have been more polite to a police officer—but this was a long, long way from being a good day.

The cop folded his arms and titled his head slightly to one side. "Would you mind telling me your name?" he asked.

Harley started to reply, then had to stop and think for a moment. As tired as she was, it took her a few seconds to remember the new name that Cain had given her. "Kathleen Vincent," she said at last.

"Vincent," the tall man repeated. He pulled out a tiny notepad and cupped it in the palm of one large hand as he scribbled down the name. "And are you from around here, Ms. Vincent?"

Harley stood up and placed the cold remains of her coffee on the bumper of the truck. "Before I answer any more questions, shouldn't I know who you are?"

The question drew a bright white smile from the man. "I suppose you should." He slipped one hand inside the lapels of his suit coat and came out with a slim leather wallet. A quick flick of his wrist, and the wallet flipped open to reveal a shiny gold badge. "My name is Locke," he said. "Senior Detective Locke, St. Louis Police Department."

Harley took a good look at the badge. She had already met false FBI agents and other officers that were under control of one of the secret groups. For the moment, she was willing to believe that Locke was exactly who he claimed to be, but she would stay ready in case his identity turned out to be just another falsehood in a long string of lies.

Detective Locke slipped his wallet closed and returned it to his suit coat. "Now that we've both identified ourselves, would you mind answering a few questions, Ms. Vincent?"

"What kind of questions?" asked Harley.

"Very simple questions." Locke jerked his thumb toward the smoldering wreck of the bookstore. "For instance, what were you doing in the Washington Avenue Book Emporium last night?"

Facing a three thousand–pound man, Harley thought. Killing a half-robot assassin with her own gun. Losing a friend. "What makes you think I was there?" she asked aloud.

The detective consulted his tiny note pad. "I have three witnesses who saw you leaving the building. Are you saying they were mistaken?"

Suddenly Harley began to regret not running away from the burning store as soon as she'd been able. She might not have anywhere she really wanted to go, but she heard something in the tone of Detective Locke's voice that made Harley think that her next destination might be a nice small room with nice shiny bars. Harley decided that as bad as things were, she still really didn't want to take up long-term residence in that room.

"I was in the store," she admitted. "But I was only looking for a book."

The detective nodded. "I see. Well, young lady, I don't suppose I can fault you for that, can I? Far too few people are readers these days."

"I like to read," said Harley. Cold raindrops fell from the cloudy dawn sky. "Can I go now? It's chilly out here."

Locke glanced down at his notepad. "This will only take a second longer. Now, you say you went into the bookstore to find a book."

Harley started to make a sharp reply. She was tired, and cold, and still stunned by the loss of Kenyon. She was in no mood to play games. But the harsh words died on her lips. "Yes," she answered tiredly. "I went to buy books."

"Right," replied Locke. He frowned, putting on a show of looking puzzled. "But according to those folks that saw you, Ms. Vincent, you came out the rear entrance of the store, the entrance to the basement."

Harley shrugged. "I was looking for a special book. The store clerk told me there were more books in the basement."

Detective Locke made a deep humming sound and nodded his head. "That certainly makes sense. Now there's just one little thing you need to explain." The detective turned the notebook around to face Harley and tapped the tiny page with the tip of his finger. "I've talked to several people, and they all agree that the bookstore closed at six. But you weren't seen leaving the building until after ten—the same time that the fire started."

"I . . . ," started Harley. Her words died away. She gathered her breath and spoke quickly. "I don't know anything about the fire." Harley said the words with as much force as she could manage, but even to her own ears they sounded like a lie.

The detective closed his palm-sized notebook and slid it into his pocket. His face had grown very still, and his brown eyes seemed hard as stone. "Are you certain you want to make that statement?"

Harley took an involuntary step backward and bumped against the cold metal side of the fire truck. "Am I under arrest?"

"Arrest?" Locke shook his head. "No, you're not under arrest. For now." He tipped the brim of his hat back, letting the morning light spill across the sharp panes of his face. "However, that may soon change. Tell me, Ms. Vincent, do you live in St. Louis?"

"No," Harley replied with a shake of her head. "I'm just . . . visiting."

"Really?" Detective Locke stepped closer and lowered his face until it was only inches from Harley's. "Then I suggest you extend that visit, Ms. Vincent. We have here a major fire whose cause is currently unknown, but which may turn out to be arson. We have witnesses who saw you running from the building at the time the fire began."

"I didn't—," Harley began.

"I advise you to be quiet," Locke interrupted her firmly. He paused for a moment, his eyes burning into Harley's. When he continued, the detective's voice was no more than a whisper. "Should I get even a *hint* that you are trying to leave this town, I will have you arrested and dropped into jail before you leave the airline ticket counter. Do you understand?"

Harley nodded slowly. "Yes. I understand."

"Good." Detective Locke straightened and took a step back. "Thanks for your cooperation, Ms. Vincent." He opened his hand and produced a small white business card with the skill of a magician pulling a rabbit from a hat. "Should you think of anything else you'd like to tell me, you can reach me at this number."

"Yes. All right." The detective's questions had only added to Harley's exhaustion. She pulled the card from Locke's fingers and looked down at the pavement.

"Oh," said the detective. "I almost forgot. There is one more thing."

When Harley looked up, she saw that Detective Locke was holding a small cylinder in his hand. It was a clear plastic tube, capped by metal at both ends. Inside it, a pale greenish fluid sloshed against the curving walls.

"That's mine," Harley said quickly. She reached out for the cylinder.

Locke pulled the small tube out of her reach. "Well, I suppose that settles the question of ownership." He held the tube up in front of his eyes and tilted it slowly back and forth. The liquid contents flowed from one end of the tube to the other. "This was found near the rear exit of the store. I thought it might be yours."

"It *is* mine," Harley insisted. "Are you going to give it to me?"

The detective stood motionless for a moment, then he slowly shook his head. "I'm afraid I can't do that."

"Why not?"

Locke shoved the tube into the pocket of his jacket. "We'll have to make sure that this container doesn't hold an accelerant."

Harley shook her head. "I don't even know what that is."

"Something to help a fire get started and make it

36

burn hotter," replied the detective. He raised one dark eyebrow. "I don't suppose you'd be willing to tell me what's in here?"

Artificial blood, thought Harley. The tube contained a substance that Agent Cain had running through his veins. Because of his injuries, he was terribly short of the fluid. What was in the cylinder might be enough to save Cain's life. "It's for a friend," she said. "I have to have it."

Locke nodded. "We'll see about that. Should it pass testing, it'll be returned to you." The detective touched one finger to the brim of his hat. "Good day, Ms. Vincent. Keep yourself handy." He turned and walked away, his shoes crunching over broken glass.

Thunder rumbled softly overhead, and the cold rain began to fall with more force. Harley turned her face up and let the cold drops wash away dirt and soot. But nothing could wash away the tangle of mournful feelings that stained her heart.

She lowered her eyes from the heavens and took one last look toward the smoking ruins. The fire was out. Only thin streamers of steam rose above the heap of blackened bricks and broken stones.

Harley turned and began to stride away, swiping at a tear trailing down her cheek. She had the detective's card clutched in her left hand, and a single thought lodged in her mind.

Kenyon is dead.

The manhole cover lifted a fraction of an inch, then settled back with a clang. For a few seconds, the street was still, then the iron cover rattled and moved again. This time, the heavy circle of metal rose higher and higher and was finally flipped away, releasing streamers of thick, reeking fog that drifted up into the cool morning air.

A dirty, trembling hand emerged through the round opening and fumbled at the pavement. A moment later, a second hand came through. Groaning with effort, Kenyon Moor climbed from the dark recesses of the storm sewer.

He pulled himself through the manhole and collapsed on the wet blacktop. For long minutes, Kenyon lay on the road with raindrops splashing around him. After escaping from Mr. Antolin's labyrinth under the bookstore, he had found himself in a seemingly endless maze of brick and concrete sewer tunnels. For hours, he had wandered in the darkness. In some places the passages had narrowed until he was forced to crawl on hands and knees through disgustingly foul liquid waste. In other spots he passed through chambers where his voice echoed back from distant walls. He had fallen, run into obstacles, and found himself at a plain old dead ends so many times that he'd lost count. By the time he saw the dull circle of light filtering down around the manhole, he had begun to think he would never get out.

Kenyon heard a screech of rubber, followed by the blare of a car horn and a splash of brown water.

He raised his head. After hours in nearly absolute darkness, even the rainy dawn sky was almost two bright for him to tolerate. He squinted through his fingers and found himself staring straight into the grillwork of an old Chevy. The front wheels of the car were no more than three feet from his body.

A man leaned through the window of the car. "Are you crazy?" the driver shouted. "Or just drunk?" Without waiting for an answer, the man pulled his head back into his car. A few seconds later, the Chevy backed up with a squeal of spinning tires, turned to the side, and sloshed away down the rain-soaked road.

Kenyon sat up and looked around him. The manhole he had escaped through was located right in the middle of a small side street. None of the buildings around him looked familiar. The bookstore that he and Harley had entered had been in the center of a business district, surrounded by tall modern buildings. Instead of skyscrapers, the street around the manhole was lined by dark brick houses.

He climbed to his feet beside the manhole and

turned slowly around. After so long wandering in the dark, Kenyon had lost all concept of direction. He had no idea which was the right way back to the bookstore, and he could see no sign of the tall buildings. He started to turn around again, then stopped. He couldn't see any familiar landmarks, but he quickly spotted a thin streamer of smoke rising up in the distance. Kenyon stepped up onto the sidewalk, and began to walk toward the source of the smoke.

Within a block, thunder rippled overhead and the drizzle increased to a downpour. At first Kenyon welcomed the rain. His face and clothes were stained by soot, sweat, blood, and the filthy water of the storm sewers. The cold rain was a poor substitute for a hot shower and a gallon of disinfectant, but at least it was something. Streams of muddy water sluiced down Kenyon's face and arms and clots of mud dropped from his pants legs. He felt a little cleaner, but it didn't take long for the chilly rain to feel simply cold. Kenyon wrapped his arms around himself and shivered as he walked.

Ten minutes of walking brought him in sight of the tall buildings of downtown St. Louis. Even in the gray light of the rainy morning, Kenyon could see the tall, elegant shape of the gateway arch standing out against the sky. Another ten minutes later, Kenyon recognized a few buildings he remembered from his trip through the city with Harley. Tired as he was, he increased his pace.

I didn't really see what happened to Harley, he told himself as he hurried through the streets. The fire might just have been in the one area. She could have gotten away. She could be . . . Kenyon's thoughts trailed off as he turned the corner and saw the place where the Washington Avenue Book Emporium had stood only the day before.

The strange, ornate building was gone. In its place was a wide depression in the ground filled with soot-stained bricks and charcoaled wood. The center of the depression was filled with a swamp of black greasy water in which nameless things floated. A score of men and women in stiff blue coveralls were searching through the rubble.

Kenyon's heart sank as he took in the incredible level of destruction. The bookstore and the labyrinth of passages that ran beneath it had not just burned, they had been completely consumed by the fire. He couldn't see one room, wall, or square foot of the building that had escaped destruction. It seemed impossible that anyone had survived this disaster.

"Over here!" shouted a woman who was standing knee-deep in the muck at the center of the wreckage. She held up her arms and waved them overhead. A pair of men holding a stretcher picked their way through the piles of debris and started down toward the woman.

Kenyon felt a new surge of hope. If they were bringing a stretcher, then they must have found a person. *Please*, he thought. *Please*. He pressed himself against the police barricade around the collapsed bookstore and stared down expectantly.

But when the men with the stretcher reached the woman, Kenyon's flash of hope instantly turned to despair. The thing they pulled from the rubble was a blackened husk. Kenyon could make out no sign of any features on its charred and crumbling face. He wasn't even sure there was anything that might have been a face remaining on the seared corpse.

Half sick, Kenyon turned away as the men carried the roasted remains out of the pit. He felt a painful mixture of guilt and sadness. If he had stayed with Harley, he might have been able to save her. They might have gotten out together. She wouldn't be . . . dead.

Even as the thoughts were passing through Kenyon's mind, his emotions were changing. His hands tightened into fists. His jaw tightened.

It's not my fault, he thought. Not my fault at all.

It was the secret organizations—those hidden masters that pulled the strings of governments and people around the world. It didn't matter if it was Unit 17 with their military uniforms and high-tech weapons, Umbra with their mysticism, or Legion with their strange mental powers. They were all the same to Kenyon—nothing but collections of monsters who would do anything or kill anyone to keep their hold on power.

Cain had said his group was different. They were

only supposed to watch and make sure that none of the other groups gained too much power. But that had been a lie. The remains of the bookstore proved that.

Kenyon's parents had been killed when they dared to cross Unit 17. Now Harley was dead because of some meaningless fight within Cain's group.

Grief and shame were burned away as Kenyon added the fuel of Harley's death to the blaze of his terrible anger. She had been killed by the secret groups, and those groups would pay for her death. Kenyon would dedicate his life to that end.

He whirled away from the destroyed store and stomped off down the street. Men and women on their way to work swerved around him on the sidewalk, and more than one stared at his soiled, torn clothing. Kenyon barely noticed. Consumed by his anger, he no longer felt the cold rain that slashed down from overhead. Without regard to his appearance, he marched straight into the lobby of a gleaming new glass-and-marble hotel. A woman in a red dress let out a startled cry as Kenyon stormed past, and another gave him a look of utter disgust. Kenyon paid no attention. He spotted a bank of telephones and advanced across the polished floor of the lobby, leaving a trail of mud and ash in his wake.

He was halfway across the lobby when a concierge in a crisp black suit headed him off. "Excuse me, *sir*," said the man. The way he said *sir* made it sound like the worst kind of insult. "I'm afraid I'm going to have to ask you to leave the Hotel Collier."

Kenyon glanced down at his clothing, then up at the concierge. "I'm just going to use the phone."

The concierge sniffed and wrinkled his lips beneath his small mustache. "Yes, well, those phones are for the use of our guests. You'll have to go elsewhere."

"I don't think so," Kenyon said with a shake of his head. He took a step past the man.

"Sir!" The man grabbed Kenyon by the arm.

Kenyon looked down at the man's fingers on his arm. "Do you know who I am?"

The concierge rolled his eyes. "I'm sure you're the King of Prussia," he said in a voice dripping with sarcasm.

"Not quite," replied Kenyon. He grasped the concierge's arm by the wrist, flipped it around, and pushed it up behind the man's back. The manager let out a squeak of pain.

"My name is Kenyon Moor. I'm the primary owner of Moor Construction. If you check your records, I believe you'll find that my company built this hotel. I own it."

"Sir, I—"

"Shut up," Kenyon interrupted calmly. "Now, I'm going to let you go, and I'm going to go over there and use the telephone. And if you get any bright ideas, remember this—you touched me first. You say one more word to me, and I'm going to have you arrested for assault." He released his grip and pushed the man away.

The concierge's face had gone whiter than the marble of the lobby. He rubbed his wrist and looked at Kenyon in shock. He kept his mouth shut.

Kenyon reached the phones and dialed quickly, tapping out the number for the mansion he owned near Stone Harbor. It took only a moment for the phone to begin ringing. It rang once. Twice. "Come on," Kenyon said under his breath. "Answer the phone."

The phone rang on and on. Kenyon scowled at the receiver. Scott and Dee should still have been at the house. Kenyon had left them in charge, with instructions to take care of the injured Agent Cain. The last time Kenyon had contacted them, Scott had admitted that Cain had escaped, but Scott had said nothing about leaving the house. After a dozen rings, Kenyon gave up in disgust and slammed the phone back on the cradle.

He stood for a moment, thinking through his next move. Just before the explosion that started the destruction of Mr. Antolin's underground home, Dee's face had appeared on the computer screens that had ringed the torture chamber. Somehow, Dee and Scott must have broken into Antolin's computer system. To manage that feat, they must have used the collection of computers at Kenyon's house. But where were they now?

"Cain," Kenyon muttered. If Dee and Scott were

missing, it probably had something to do with Agent Cain. Kenyon had never trusted the agent. If Cain had escaped, he might have done anything. He might even have gone back after Scott and Dee.

His anger now tinged with panic, Kenyon reached for the phone again and dialed the number for the beach house where Harley had been staying. Both Dee and Scott had been visitors at the house. They might have gone there.

While the phone was ringing, he glanced across the lobby and saw that someone was standing beside one of the leather couches, staring back at him. That wasn't too surprising. Half the people in the lobby were casting dismayed glances at the filthy young man by the phones. Only this person didn't seem to be upset, and her look was not embarrassed.

She was a tall woman with dark hair and olive skin, and she was wearing a smooth, white linen dress that perfectly offset the rich tan of her skin. A scarf of blue silk held back her thick hair. Though there were dark sunglasses on her face, Kenyon had no doubt that the woman was looking straight at him.

The woman raised up her sunglasses, revealing eyes of deep brown. She stared at Kenyon for a moment longer, then let the glasses fall back into place and turned away.

Kenyon hung up the phone and started across the lobby toward the woman. There was something about her. Something familiar.

He had taken only a few steps before the woman

strode swiftly across the lobby and disappeared through a revolving door. Kenyon followed. He pressed through the door and came out onto the sidewalk so fast that he was almost flung into the street.

There was no sign of the woman.

The rainy street was relatively deserted, and Kenyon could see down the street for blocks in either direction, but the woman in white had completely disappeared. He was about to give up and return to the phones when he spotted an envelope lying on the wet sidewalk at his feet. It was a large, buff-colored envelope with a string binding the flap closed. Written in neat letters on the exposed surface was the phrase "For K. M."

With one last glance around, Kenyon bent and picked up the envelope. Drops of water rolled from its surface as he raised it from the ground, but the paper had not soaked through. As hard as it was raining, the envelope must only have been there for seconds.

Kenyon brought the package back into the hotel. Cautiously, he held the envelope up to the ceiling lamps and tried to peer through it. He knew that an envelope this size could hold enough high explosives to level a small building, but if a letter bomb was waiting inside, he couldn't tell.

He grabbed the string holding the flap closed and unwound it. Carefully, he opened the end of the envelope. Kenyon saw nothing inside but a few sheets of glossy paper.

Fumbling with his damp, dirty fingers, Kenyon pulled out a page. Only a few lines were centered on the sheet, and from the poor quality of the printing, it looked like a bad copy of a poorly transmitted fax, but Kenyon could make out most of the words.

COLLECT DAVISIDARO .N. ALL OTHERS WITH KNOWL.D.GE MAKE SURE ALL CONTACTS COVE . . . ED STONE HARBOR TO .E SANITIZED.

Kenyon read the short message a dozen times. It seemed to be someone ordering the capture—possibly the death—of Harley and her friends. He thought it was quite possible that this was the message that had sent the killer Till after Harley. But the page gave no clue as to who had issued the order.

The second sheet as badly garbled as the first. But the message was clear enough.

UNDE.STOOD WI.L SECURE TRUST O. DAVISI.ARO MAK. SURE WE HAV. T.EM ALL IN TH. TRAP BEFORE WE CLOSE T.E DOOR

Overall, the two messages were much alike—with one big difference. At the bottom of the second message there was a scrawled signature. Kenyon had no trouble making out the name.

Ian Cain.

Harley listened to the phone ring for the twentieth time, then jammed it back onto its cradle. She had tried to reach Dee and Scott at Kenyon's mansion, and at the beach house, but had no luck.

On one level she was worried. Dee and Scott had managed to break into Mr. Antolin's computer system, and the distraction they caused had helped Harley to escape, but that had been hours ago. Anything could have happened since then. They could be in trouble. But Harley also felt a certain amount of relief. She had done her duty and tried to call. If they weren't home, she didn't have to give them the bad news about Kenyon.

Harley stepped away from the phone booth and joined the crowd of people moving along the street. She really had no particular destination in mind. With Kenyon dead and everyone else out of touch, Harley couldn't think of anywhere she wanted to be. She felt an odd, disconnected sensation. People hurried by on all sides of her, but Harley knew none of them. Her dirty, soot-stained clothing drew some glances, but most of the people simply ignored her. She felt as detached from these people as a ghost, as though she was slowly fading into invisibility.

A small park appeared on the right. It was too

early in the year for flowers, though the green shoots of daffodils were beginning to peek through the dark earth. Harley found an empty bench under the bare branches of a maple tree and sat down. Water dripped slowly down on her from the branches of the tree, but it felt good just to be sitting.

For a moment, she thought of taking a nap on the park bench. It was daylight, and there were a lot of people around. Someone might be upset about her sleeping there, but at least it wasn't likely that she would be mugged. Then she had another idea—if she wasn't connected to anyone in the world, maybe she could connect to someone who was in another.

Harley squeezed her eyes shut tight and searched for a spark of light behind her eyelids. "Noah," she whispered under her breath.

A tiny pinprick of faint illumination appeared in the darkness. Harley pressed herself toward the light, using muscles she couldn't name as she swam through the murk of her own mind. But no matter how hard she tried, the light stayed distant. Finally, the spark began to fade. In moments, it was lost.

A fresh wave of despair washed over Harley and threatened to drown her in a sea of depression. She had lost her father, and Noah, and now Kenyon. It didn't seem fair.

She opened her eyes and looked at the grassy lawn in front of her. It *wasn't* fair. None of what had happened to her was fair, but that didn't stop it from happening. One thing was absolutely sure—sitting around and feeling sorry for herself was not going to make things better.

As if she were lifting a physical weight, Harley shoved her despair aside. She pressed her lips together in grim determination. Kenyon might be dead, but she was still alive. She had to get in touch with Scott and Dee to let them know what had happened. She had to find Cain and see if he was all right. She had to find the people that were behind the secret groups and see that they didn't get a chance to mess up anyone else's life the way they had hers. It was time to get to work.

Harley dug into the tight pocket of her scuffed leather pants and came out with a tiny roll of crumpled bills. Even without counting, she knew it was far too small an amount for an airplane ticket, even at the cheapest discount airline. She fingered the ragged bills. She might have enough for a bus or train ticket. Stone Harbor was all the way over on the East Coast, over a thousand miles away. Harley doubted she had enough to travel all the way home, but at least she could get closer.

With a glimmer of a plan in mind, Harley stood up, brushed some of the dirt off her soiled sweater, and began walking. It took her only a few minutes to locate a tiny Amtrak station crammed under an overpass. She joined a line of people waiting in the ticket line and scanned the list of departures. Naturally, there was no train going to Stone Harbor, but there was a four o'clock departure that headed east to

Ohio. That would get Harley halfway to where she wanted to go.

The line of passengers advanced forward briskly. Harley clutched her small supply of cash in her hands and hoped it would be enough.

The woman ticket agent glanced up as Harley reached the counter. "Where you going, honey?" the woman asked.

"Um, Cincinnati," Harley replied.

"First class or coach?"

"Coach. Definitely coach."

The woman tapped some keys on a computer terminal. "All right. That'll be forty-eight fifty."

Harley winced. Buying the ticket would leave her with less than two dollars. Once she got to Ohio, she would have to find some other source of cash, or some cheaper way to travel. Once thing was sure— she wouldn't be eating any of the five-dollar hot dogs in the dining car. Grudgingly, she unfolded her money and held it out toward the woman.

A hand clamped down on Harley's wrist.

"I thought we agreed you were staying in St. Louis," growled a deep voice at her side.

Harley looked up to see Detective Locke glaring down at her. The expression on the detective's face was not happy. "What are you doing here?" she asked.

"Stopping a suspect from leaving the state," Locke replied. He took his hand from Harley's wrist, then leaned in close to her and lowered his voice. "Come along with me, and we won't have to do anything that might upset these people."

Harley gritted her teeth and followed the detective to the door of the train station. "How did you know where to find me?"

"That was easy enough," replied Locke. He paused and opened the door for Harley. "I had you followed."

Harley felt a flash of anger—not at Locke, but at herself. She had been so busy moping and whining that she hadn't been paying attention. She glanced warily around the train station. She was willing to bet that the undercover cop who had followed her to the station was still nearby, but she still couldn't spot him in the crowd. If it had been a Unit 17 agent after her instead of a cop, she would have been cut into ribbons by now.

She stepped through the door and into the gray afternoon. The detective followed close behind.

Outside the train station, a brown sedan waited in the gravel parking lot. Locke crunched across the lot and opened the back door. "Get in," he said simply.

Harley stared out across the rows of parked cars. She thought for a moment of running. She was tired, and the detective had much longer legs than she did, but Harley had been training as a runner almost since she was old enough to walk. She was willing to bet she'd outrun the detective in a race of any distance.

"Now are you arresting me?" she asked.

Locke paused beside the car and seemed to consider this question. "I will if I have to," he replied. "I'd prefer it if you came in on your own and talked with me, but I believe we have the evidence we need."

"What evidence?"

The detective nodded toward the car. "Get in," he said. "We'll discuss it on the way to the station."

Harley bit her lip. She gave another moment's thought to running. It would be a relief to just get away from St. Louis and everything that had happened here. On the other hand, it would mean that Kathleen Vincent would have a *real* police record to compliment the fake police record of Kathleen Davisidaro. She would be stuck with two identities, both of them wanted for crimes she never committed.

Harley might be able to outrun the detective, but she didn't want to keep running forever. "All right," she said. "Let's go." Harley climbed into the back of the car.

"A very good decision," replied Locke. He shut the door behind her, walked around to the front, and slipped behind the wheel. Gravel clanked against the fenders of the car as he sped out of the parking lot.

A mesh of heavy metal wire separated the front seat of the sedan from the back. Harley turned to the side and noticed that there were no door handles on the inside. People who sat in the backseat of this car were trapped until the police let them out.

"We're in the car," said Harley.

"What's that?" the detective asked over his shoulder.

Harley leaned forward, bringing her face close to the dented metal screen. "We're in the car," she repeated. "You said you'd talk about the evidence when we got into the car."

"I suppose I did." Harley saw Locke's brown eyes reflected in the rearview mirror as the detective glanced back at her. "Tell me, Ms. Vincent, who else was in that basement with you?"

The question brought a hard lump to Harley's throat. She shook her head. "No one," she replied in a hoarse voice.

Locke made a noise that might have been a hard laugh, but there was no humor in the sound. "Don't lie to me. I can't help you if you lie to me."

Harley blinked in surprise. "Help me? I didn't know you were trying to help me."

"Don't get me wrong," said the detective. His large hands slid across the wheel as he steered the car down a narrow street between two brick warehouses. "My first task is to solve this crime. If I think you're behind it, I'll do whatever I can to see you convicted."

Harley leaned back against the split and faded vinyl of the seat. She turned the detective's words over in her head, trying to decide how far she could trust this man. "You don't think I did it," she said slowly.

Detective Locke shrugged his big shoulders. "Nope. Call it a hunch, but I don't think so."

"Why not?"

A traffic light turned red just ahead of them. Locke brought the car to a halt, the turned around to look directly at Harley. "Because, Ms. Vincent, you don't strike me as a murderer."

The word struck Harley like a kick. "Murderer?"

The detective nodded. "The fire crews have already pulled two victims out of the Book Emporium. They're now looking for more."

Two bodies. "Can you . . ." The lump in Harley's throat turned into a burning mass that made it almost impossible to speak. She swallowed hard and tried again. "Can you tell me anything about the bodies you found?"

"Not at the moment." Locke tapped his fingers against the seat of the car. "Maybe you can tell me something. How many people were down in that basement with you?"

Harley hesitated. If she admitted seeing anyone in the basement, she was willing to bet it would lead to a million other questions. But if she said she was alone, Kenyon's body might never be identified. Somewhere out there, Kenyon had a brother. Kenyon's brother had been suing him to stop him from using up the family fortune, but that didn't mean there was no love between them. There were probably other family members that Harley didn't even know about, people who would care that Kenyon was gone.

Harley knew what it was like to have people you loved just disappear. The least she could do was give Kenyon's family a chance for a proper funeral.

"There was a friend with me in the bookstore," she said quickly.

The traffic light turned green, but Locke didn't move. He continued to look at Harley over the back of his car seat. "Does this friend have a name?"

Harley nodded. "Kenyon . . . Kenyon Moor."

A car horn sounded from behind them. Detective Locke glanced at the rear window, then back at Harley. "Tell me, Ms. Vincent, is this friend of yours very interested in chemistry?"

The question was so strange that it caught Harley by complete surprise. "Chemistry?"

"Or was that you?" asked Locke. "Maybe you're a real wizard with a test tube."

Harley shook her head. "I don't know what you're talking about."

The car behind them honked again. Detective Locke glared back, and his calm expression was momentarily transformed into a snarl. "Some idiots never know when to go around," he muttered under his breath. His eyes shifted to Harley. "Tell me, were you cooking the drugs, or did you just go there to make a buy?"

"Drugs?" Harley felt a very inappropriate laugh coming on and pushed it away with an effort. "What are you talking about?"

"Believe it or not," replied Locke, "the police

department is not staffed with total idiots. In the remains of that bookstore, we've found dozens of metal vats, broken glassware, and medical supplies. There was enough high-tech gear down there to make a billion dollars worth of designer drugs." His dark eyebrows lowered. "Or do you have another explanation for what we found?"

It was used to keep a two hundred-year-old, three thousand–pound man alive, Harley thought, but what she said was, "I don't know."

Locke nodded slowly. "You can take that position if you want, but keep this in mind—the bodies in that building change the situation. We're not talking about arson now, we're talking about *murder*." The detective turned around, put the car in gear, and drove on.

Harley let her head fall back against the cushions of the seat. Murder. The police were not going to let this one slide by easily. If Harley was going to avoid a long time in jail, she had to come up with a very good story and stick with it. She wondered what Detective Locke would think if she told him what really happened beneath the Washington Avenue Book Emporium. She suspected that the detective would waste no time calling for the men in white jackets to take Harley to a nice padded room.

Her mind drifted back over the events of the last days. She tried to weave some kind of tale out of the fragments, but everything seemed to be blurring together. The order of events fell away, and images swirled through her mind in a chaos of colors and sound.

Harley's eyes slipped closed, and she fell into a doze as the car traveled slowly through the city streets. A point of light appeared in the darkness of her mind. It grew closer, gaining warmth and brightness as it approached.

Harley's lips curved up in a smile. "Noah," she breathed.

Kenyon turned the gun over in his hands. "This is a piece of junk," he declared.

The pawnshop owner snatched the little revolver back. "Yeah? Well, you get what you pay for. You want this thing or not?"

Kenyon pulled his billfold from his khaki trousers, opened it, and surveyed the cash inside. No new money had grown since the last time he'd checked. He supposed he should be grateful that Mr. Antolin and his goons had not taken the money away. They had robbed Kenyon of the miniature computer-cell phone combination unit he had used to communicate with Scott and Dee, but nobody had touched his wallet.

In normal circumstances, Kenyon would have had enough cash on hand to purchase an arsenal. According to his accountants, his share of his parent's corporation was worth over a hundred million dollars, and he was perfectly willing to spend every penny of that fighting to destroy Unit 17 and the other secret organizations. Unfortunately, Kenyon's brother, Cameron, did not agree. Kenyon had been going through the company money at a very rapid rate. The diminishing funds had been enough to upset both Cameron and the company's officers. Kenyon's supply of cash had gone from a flood to a trickle as they managed to put a legal freeze on his assets.

"Well?" asked the pawnshop owner. He was a skinny man with a patch of hair on either side of his bald head and an impatient expression on his narrow face. "What's it going to be?"

Kenyon looked at the little nickel-plated gun and frowned. It was a pitiful weapon. Compared to the lightning device carried by Agent Cain, the revolver might as well have been a pop gun. "No," he decided with a shake of his head. "I guess not."

The pawnshop owner rolled his eyes. "Fine. Whatever." He dropped the gun back into a glass case and closed the door with a bang. "You know where it is if you want it, but next time don't waste my time till you're ready to buy. Understand?" Without waiting for an answer, the shop owner turned away from Kenyon and went to help another man waiting at the end of the counter.

Kenyon headed out of the store between racks of junk and unclaimed merchandise. A bell chimed above his head as he pushed open the door and stepped out onto the street. The rain had stopped, and the sun was beginning to burn through the clouds. The brightening sky did nothing to cheer Kenyon. As walked along the street, passing shops and restaurants, his thoughts were a million miles away.

Cain, he thought, tightening his hands into fists. It was Cain all along.

He had never trusted Cain. The so-called agent had come to Kenyon in Washington, claiming to be from the FBI. Cain had told the same story to Harley, but the whole FBI thing had turned out to be a lie. The organization that Cain served was not a part of the government, and not under the control of law or regulations. Like Unit 17, Umbra, and Legion, Cain's unnamed group ruined people's lives and answered to no one.

Several times, the agent had done things that seemed helpful, and Harley had been willing to risk herself to save the man. Kenyon had disagreed with her. He supposed the results of their attempt to help Cain had proved him right, but being right certainly didn't make him feel better. Harley had paid for her mistake with her life.

Still, Kenyon had been surprised by the contents of the letters he had found inside the brown envelope. The garbled messages left little doubt that Cain had not only been aware that Kenyon and Harley might be hurt; he had planned it that way. And for all of Cain's shady methods, Kenyon had never suspected the agent wanted them dead. From what Kenyon could understand in the series of faded notes, there never even had been a struggle for power within Cain's group. The splinter group called Tessera was nothing but an invention. Cain had created the lie to draw out Harley and everyone around her so they would be easier to eliminate.

The whole scheme seemed a little too complicated, and Kenyon was suspicious of the way the messages had come into his hands, but the notes went a long way toward explaining some of the nagging questions he had about Cain. They also explained why he hadn't been able to contact Dee or Scott. Before Kenyon and Harley had been captured by Mr. Antolin, he'd received a message from Stone Harbor that Agent Cain was missing. That was the last he'd heard from Dee and Scott before Dee had appeared on the monitors in the underground torture chamber. Since then, he hadn't heard a word.

When Kenyon and Harley had left Stone Harbor, Cain had been lying on a bed, apparently near death. He had told Harley that another agent from his organization had shot him, and he certainly seemed to be wounded. Kenyon had thought the agent was much too badly injured to move. Obviously, that had been a mistake.

Kenyon had to assume that the reason he had not been able to get in touch with Dee and Scott was because his two friends were in trouble. Cain might have returned and captured them. After Dee interrupted Caska's attempt to torture Kenyon, Cain might have *killed* both Dee and Scott.

A roaring sound rose in Kenyon's ears, and his teeth ground together so hard his jaws ached as he gave in to his anger. After his parents were so senselessly murdered, he had dedicated himself to crushing the military group called Unit 17. That mission was not over. But for the time being, another job came first.

Kenyon was going to find Agent Ian Cain. And then he would kill him. Kenyon would stop at nothing until that mission was accomplished and until Harley's death, and possibly the deaths of Dee and Scott, were avenged.

Still in a haze of anger, Kenyon found himself walking back toward the site of the burned bookstore. The fire had been out for hours now. The firefighters should be long gone. Though the destruction had been almost total, it was a place to start. If he searched through the wreckage, he might find something that would lead him to Cain.

He was within a block of the bookstore when a hand reached out from an alley, grabbed him by the arm, and jerked him from the sidewalk and into an alley.

Months of training sprang into effect. Without thinking, Kenyon whirled and kicked, delivering a blow with the edge of his foot that should have left any attacker nursing a broken leg. Instead, jarring pain ran up Kenyon's shin and left him hurting all the way to the top of his head. The grip on his arm only tightened. He looked up into the blank, midnight face of the shadow man.

"You . . ." Kenyon whispered in shock.

The shadow man's ratty clothing was gone. Now it was completely exposed for what it truly was—a thing of darkness, a man-shaped outline of night. Its fingers grabbed tighter at Kenyon's arm, freezing his flesh in its grip.

"Where is he?" the shadow man demanded in its slow, ocean-deep voice.

Kenyon bit back a scream. The thing's hold on his arm was insanely hard and cold, like a clamp made from ice. He could feel the muscles of his arm becoming increasingly frigid—turning to ice. "Who?" he cried. "Where is *who?*"

The shadow man lifted him from the ground and drew him close to the rounded patch of darkness that passed for the creature's face. Within that black gulf, a pair of red points gleamed. "Templer," it intoned. "Where is Templer?"

Kenyon's mouth dropped open in surprise. He didn't know why the creature would be asking him about Noah, and he had no time to find out. "I'll tell you," he gasped. "Just let me go."

The shadow man complied at once. It released its grip on Kenyon's left arm, letting him fall to his knees. "Where is Templer?" it asked again.

The place where the creature had touched Kenyon's arm was a frighteningly numb band in the middle of a spread of agony. The arm dangled immobile from his aching shoulder. A sensation of pins and needles tingled painfully in his hand and wrist.

"Where?" insisted the shadow man. It reached out for him again.

Kenyon drew back from the thing and scooted

into a gap between a pair of round metal trash cans. "Templer's gone," he answered.

The shadow man took a step forward. "Gone where?"

"Just gone," Kenyon replied. He stole a quick glance down the alley. He saw nothing except rows of trash Dumpsters, blowing paper, and pair of fire escapes far overhead. At least the alley continued as far as he could see. If he could get loose, he would have somewhere to run.

A low, throbbing growl issued from the shadow man. "Tell," it said. "Where is Templer?"

"Right over there," said Kenyon. He pointed toward the mouth of the alley.

The dark creature was terribly strong, but that didn't mean it was all that bright. It turned its head in the direction that Kenyon had pointed out. "Templer?" it asked.

Kenyon grabbed the lid from one of the trash cans, cocked his arm, and sailed the circle of metal right into the shadow man's throat. Before the missile had a chance to strike home, he jumped to his feet, pulled over the two trash cans, and sprinted away down the alley.

Behind him, Kenyon heard the trash can lid bounce from the shadow man's body with a sound like a hammer beating on a sheet of tin. He didn't even turn to look. After the blows that Kenyon had seen the creature take and still survive, he had no doubt it would shrug off this attack. He only hoped it would slow the creature down until he could find a more effective weapon.

There was a banging and crunching as the shadow man pushed its way past the fallen trash cans. Then there was a solid *thump-thump-thump* as the creature began to run. The shadow man was certainly no sprinter, but Kenyon had an idea that the creature might be able to keep up its pace for a long, long time. In the end, he couldn't outrun the shadow man. He would have to face it, fight it, and kill it.

As he sprinted down the alley, Kenyon searched his memory, trying to remember if anyone had told him of a way to kill these dark creatures. If he remembered correctly, lightning guns, like the one carried by Cain, were effective against the shadow men. That might mean that any form of electricity would work. He looked to his right and scanned the passing walls of the alley, his breath already becoming labored. Kenyon saw a few cables low enough to reach, but those looked like either cable television or telephone lines, neither of which was likely to damage the shadow man.

The creature was gaining on him. He could hear its heavy footsteps growing closer. If he was going to defeat the shadow man, he was going to have to find something fast.

When his chance came, he almost passed it by. In fact, he did run past, but a half dozen paces further on, he spun around and dashed back to the object he had seen coiled against the base of the alley wall.

It was a simple garden hose, grass green, with a nozzle of shiny brass. Kenyon fumbled to uncoil the hose from the wall and turn on the water. The shadow man lumbered closer with every pounding step, and Kenyon's left hand was all but useless from the creature's freezing touch.

The shadow man was within twenty feet of him by the time Kenyon was ready. He gave the valve on the wall a single, desperate spin. Then he whirled around and aimed a jet of clear water at the creature's chest.

The water never reached the shadow man. Inches away from the black form, the spray turned into a froth of ice. The ice thumped against the creature's chest. And it stuck. Within moments a jacket of ice covered the shadow man from shoulder to knee. The shadow man stumbled to a halt and gave a deep, rumbling cry. It raised one dark fist and battered at the frozen casing on its chest. Chunks of blue, cold ice and motes of impossible snow flew away, exposing the thing's dark skin, but Kenyon kept the spray coming.

He fumbled at the tap with his aching left hand and managed to open the valve even further. The increased spray spread ice across the shadow man's arms, legs, and face.

The coating enraged the creature. It moaned and thrashed, throwing ice in all directions, even as Kenyon added layer after of layer to its burden.

"Come on," he called to it. "See how *you* like being frozen."

The monster lowered its arms and stumbled forward. Inches of glaze covered its face and neck. Thick icicles clung along its arms and more ice ran in irregular miniglaciers along the creature's legs. Water on the floor of the alley hissed, popped, and froze as the shadow man shuffled forward.

Kenyon kept the water flowing. He built a helmet of ice around the thing's head and formed a shell around its torso that dripped down like a translucent raincoat.

But despite a burden of ice that must have weighed hundreds of pounds, the shadow man kept staggering toward Kenyon. It gave up trying to free itself and simply shuffled forward, shedding sheets of ice at every step.

As the creature drew near, Kenyon was forced to retreat one step, then another. He backed down the alley, still holding the end of the hose and still directing the stream of water toward the thing's head. "Freeze," he told it. "Just freeze."

The water suddenly stopped.

Kenyon squeezed desperately on the nozzle, but only a tiny drip came out. Then he glanced down and saw that the shadow man had stepped on the hose. In an instant, its touch had frozen the water inside, ruining Kenyon's weapon.

The shadow man threw out its right arm and smashed it against the brick wall of the alley. Kenyon was bombarded by chunks and chips of broken ice. Then the shadow man raised its dark hand and brought it savagely down against its own featureless face.

The blow sounded like an ax biting into wood. Fragments of ice the size of baseballs went flying through the air, and Kenyon staggered as a smaller chunk bounced from his temple. He turned, started to run, and put his foot down on one of the fragments of frozen water.

Kenyon's feet flew out from under him. He fell heavily to the ice-strewn pavement.

Before he could rise, midnight black fingers closed on the front of his shirt. Kenyon was hoisted off the ground and held like a doll in front of the shadow man. "Where is Templer?" it demanded. For the first time, Kenyon thought he heard emotion in the creature's rumbling voice—a hint of anger.

"I know where he is," Kenyon replied. His own anger dropped over him—his cold rage, in its own way, every bit as icy as the shadow man's darkness. "But I'm not going to tell you or your boss." He spit into the thing's face, leaving a frozen glob of saliva plastered to its dark head.

The shadow man rumbled wordlessly. It raised its other dark hand and pressed it to the skin of Kenyon's neck.

Kenyon threw back his head in agony as the cold began to freeze his throat, his blood, his life.

Then the world rippled.

A space of pure chaos flew past Kenyon's head and struck the shadow man in the chest. The creature lost its hold on Kenyon and spun back along the alley as though it had been struck by a cannonball. The shadow man crashed down on top of a Dumpster and lay still. Frost spread out across the metal in an outline of the thing's black form.

Kenyon lay on the ground and tried to make some sense out of what he had seen. *Something* had whooshed past him and flattened the shadow man. He had seen it, heard it, smelled it, felt it—sensed it with his whole body. But he couldn't begin to describe the experience. In part, it was like the haze that rises above a hot road on a summer day, and the tingling sensation of a leg that has fallen asleep, and the little *something* that scuttles just out of sight in dark corners of old houses. But none of that came close.

"You had better get up," said a woman's voice.

Still stunned, Kenyon turned his head and saw the woman who had left the envelope for him back at the hotel. "Who—who are you?" he asked. He sat up and rubbed a hand across his nearly frostbitten throat.

The woman stood over Kenyon for a moment, staring down with her dark brown eyes. "That's not important right now," she said calmly. Her heavy, dark hair had been bound in a long, thick braid that fell over her shoulder as she looked down. Instead of the white dress she had been wearing at the hotel, she was wearing loose, dark clothing that glistened like silk around her slender form. "What's important is that this weapon only has one shot," she said. "If you want to get out of here, you better do it now."

As if to punctuate her words, there was a groan from down the alley. Kenyon turned his head and saw that the shadow man was sitting up. Slowly and deliberately, the dark creature climbed to its feet.

"Here," said the woman. "This will tell you what you need to know." She dropped a square of cardboard into Kenyon's lap, then stepped over his outstretched legs as she walked down the alley toward the shadow man. She shook back the sleeves of her clothing, exposing her hands and forearms. For the first time, Kenyon noticed that her feet were bare.

Kenyon picked up the card. "Wait," he called to the woman. "What are you doing?"

"Buying time," she replied without turning. "Now, *go*. Hurry."

The words were barely out of her mouth before she broke into a run. Her feet flew across the floor of the alley, skillfully avoiding the fragments of melting ice. She ran straight toward the shadow man.

Kenyon scrambled to his feet. "Look out!" he cried. "You can't fight that thing!"

The strange woman ignored him. Twenty feet away from the shadow man, she suddenly jumped into the air, landed on her hands, then sprang forward, driving both feet into the creature's unseen face.

Kenyon had trained with black belt instructors in three kinds of martial arts, but the force and speed of the woman's blow was like beyond anything he had ever seen. Any human being who had received such a kick would be a human being in search of a new head.

Even the shadow man was staggered by the energy of the attack. It stumbled back a step, then raised a huge hand to squash its attacker. But the woman wasn't there when the blow arrived.

She bounced away from the shadow man, rolled under its arm, and spun around to deliver a round-house kick to the back of the creature's knee. The shadow man fell to the ground.

Kenyon stood there and watched in awe as the woman danced in to deliver a kick to the creature's head, then a sharp punch, then another kick. Crusts of ice formed across her knuckles and her bare feet, but the woman never slowed. Every blow was impossibly fast and brutally hard. Her hands would have turned bricks to powder. Her feet would have dented steel.

The woman glanced down the alley. "Don't stand there with your mouth open!" she shouted. "Run!"

Kenyon didn't move, unable to stop watching as the shadow man managed to grab the woman's feet. She was thrown back. The shadow man climbed to a standing position, and a sound like thunder emerged from its throat as it lunged toward her.

The woman sprang up, pirouetted in place, then ran down the alley away from Kenyon with blinding speed. Still rumbling in outrage, the shadow man followed.

Kenyon stumbled after them. He caught one glimpse of the shadow man lumbering into the mouth of a crossing alley, but by the time he reached the intersection, there was no sign of either of the combatants. He stood in the center of the alley for long minutes. The image of the mysterious woman would not leave his mind. He kept seeing the way her loose, soft clothing had draped around her as she moved, and the flashing, powerful way she had fought the creature.

Finally, Kenyon thought to glance down at the card he was holding in his hand. There was no name. No phone number. Written in simple, clean handwriting was a place and a time.

Kenyon scanned the card again and put it in his pocket. This was one appointment he was not about to miss.

SIX

The grass on the hillside was so tall that Harley could barely see over it.

She held out her hands in front of her and pressed through the smooth stalks. The grass hissed softly as she brushed past. Green stains formed on the palms of Harley's hands, and a golden dust of pollen settled on her dark hair. Around her there was a soft buzz of a million insects going about their spring business. The warm air was heavy with the sweet scent of nearby blossoms.

"Noah?" she called hopefully. "Noah, are you here?" She heard no reply but the whine of the insects and the faint sound of the wind whispering its way over the field.

The field of tall grass extended for perhaps half a mile. When the lush growth began to thin, Harley found herself facing a curving wall of forest. The trees were huge—so big that she could not have wrapped her arms around the smallest trunk. Their limbs were gnarled by weather and age and spotted over with gray-green patches of lichen. At the edge of the forest, wildflowers grew in profusion. A riot of red, blue, white, and yellow blossoms pressed in along roots of the big trees. Jonquils, irises, crocuses, daisies, and wild violets all crowded together more closely than in any florist's display. Bees, heavily laden with the makings of honey, buzzed slowly from flower to flower.

Harley stood there for a moment, savoring the sunshine at the edge of the wood. In one part of her mind, she knew that the fields, the flowers, and the forests weren't real. Not *really* real, like Detective Locke's grungy car and the smoking ruins of the Washington Avenue Book Emporium. But another part of Harley's mind insisted that this place was real, or at least *should* be real.

She drew in one last breath of the sweet air from the meadow, then stepped in among the trees. Away from the forest's edge the masses of flowers gave way to scattered clumps of bluebells, May apples, and Indian paintbrush. Birds flitted among the lower limbs of the ancient trees. Overhead, the wind passed through the branches with a soft rustling.

Drawn by some nameless instinct, Harley followed a twisting path between the dark trunks. Out of the sunlight, the air was crisp, even a little chilly. Harley wrapped her arms around herself and shivered as she walked on past broad off-white mushrooms and thick dangling vines. Gradually, the forest ahead began to brighten. The odor of wood smoke joined the damp, musky smell of the forest, and Harley noticed a distant, regular ringing sound, like a hammer pounding on metal.

Harley emerged from the forest and found herself atop a green hillside. Fields of green wheat and young corn spread down the slope before her. In the valley below was a tight cluster of small houses and log buildings. White curls of smoke emerged from a dozen chimneys, and everything seemed well cared for, but she saw no people in the tiny village.

"Harley!" a voice shouted from below.

She turned to the side and saw Noah Templer hiking toward her up the slope. He held one hand over his head and waved.

Harley smiled and waved back. She waited there at the edge of the forest as Noah drew closer.

Several times since he had stepped into the white sphere generated by Unit 17, Noah had contacted Harley in her dreams. The last time they had talked had been only hours before, right after Harley had been thrown from the bookstore by an explosion. In those hours, Noah had changed. His blond hair was longer. It fell over his ears and brushed against his shoulders as he walked. He wore no shirt, and the smooth skin of his muscled chest and shoulders was tanned several shades darker than Harley remembered. Even his clothing had changed. Instead of the jeans he had worn when he went into the sphere, he wore pants of a rough, brown weave that ended just below his knees.

Noah ran the last hundred yards to meet her. He skidded to a stop in front of Harley, took both her hands in his, and drew her against him. "I've missed you," he said softly, his face buried in Harley's hair. "It's been so long."

"So long?" Harley pulled back slightly. "But we talked less than a day ago. How can you have changed so much in a day?"

Noah shrugged. "Time's . . . funny. In here it goes slow sometimes, fast others. For me it's been a lot longer than a day."

"How long has it been for you?"

"Too long." Noah drew Harley against him again and wrapped his arms around her.

Harley felt her skin warm against Noah. She closed her eyes and pressed her face into the hollow of his neck. "This seems so real," she murmured. "Is it real?"

"I've been working on it," Noah whispered into her ear. "I've been learning."

Harley opened her eyes and stepped back. Behind Noah the wind was moving over the fields. It whipped the top of the wheat stems in waves like a sea during a storm. A hawk launched itself from the branches of a tree and sailed upward on the wind with its wings spread wide.

Harley laughed and shook her head. "The last time we were together, the woods and the village felt like something out of a movie. But now . . ." She shook her head again. "This is no movie. This is real. This is perfect."

Noah made a slight bow. "Thanks," he said. "I aim to please."

"Are we inside the sphere?"

"Sort of." Noah frowned. "You asked that once

before, and I'm afraid I still don't have a good answer." He gestured at the fields around them. "This place is a model. It's based on the place where I am, but its not exactly the same."

Harley considered his words for a moment. "Which parts are the same?"

Noah frowned, then laughed. "Absolutely nothing. Look, Harley, I can't explain what it's like inside the sphere. I've been in here for, well . . . for what seems like a long time, and I still don't even know how to start telling you what it's like."

Harley bit her lip. "Does it hurt?"

"No, I'm okay," Noah replied. He reached out and stroked Harley's hair. "Listen, we can't stay here much longer. I need to talk to you about something while there's still time."

Harley sighed. The pleasant green fields and the little village seemed so much better than anything she had to go back to. "I don't want to leave this place," she said. "Can't we just stay here?"

Noah shook his head. "No. I'm sorry, but no."

"What about my father?" asked Harley. "Is he with you?"

Noah's smile faded. He turned and looked away across the fields. "No," he said. "Your father's not with me."

Harley felt a surge of black despair. The Unit 17 leader, Commander Braddock, had shot Harley's father just before Braddock was himself pulled into the sphere. There had been no way her father could live with the wound in the normal world, but Harley had hoped her father might find some kind of healing inside the sphere.

"Is he dead?" she asked.

Noah shook his head. "No, he's not dead."

Harley gave a puzzled frown. "Then what's wrong?"

A bank of clouds suddenly rose in the sky with supernatural speed. The warm sunlight vanished and the temperature of the air seemed to drop thirty degrees in an instant.

"Quickly," said Noah. "Let me tell you what I know."

"What about my father?" Harley asked.

"Not now." He reached again for Harley's hand. "This is important."

"More important that my father?"

An enormous, bell-like sound rang over the fields. With the noise, the whole world shook around Harley. When the noise had passed, everything around her seemed slicker, flatter—less real. The bell tolled again. The ground rippled under the noise. A gray fog appeared at the edge of the valley and began to move quickly inward. The little village and the neat fields vanished behind the spreading gray blanket.

Noah pulled Harley close. "Stay with me!" he shouted. "This is important!"

"What is it?" Harley asked, panic fluttering in her chest. "What's going on?"

"Interference!" Noah shouted. "It's—"

The bell sounded a third time. All color faded from the world as the gray fog passed over Harley. For a moment, she could still feel Noah pressed close against her. Then even that feeling began to fade. Her grip slipped through his as though she was trying to hold onto a handful of sand.

"Noah!" she shouted.

The bell sang again, only this time the noise was not as loud and the pitch was higher. It came again. And again. With each sounding, the volume of the bell decreased and became sharper, until it reminded Harley of a long series of metallic clicks.

Harley snapped awake to see bars in front of her face. A young gum-chewing policeman was dragging a billy club across the bars from the other side, raising the series of clicks she had been hearing.

"So, the sleeping princess is awake," said the policeman. He gave the bars a final rap, then slipped the club into a holder at his belt.

Harley sat up and looked around. She was in a small cell, with a single hard bunk and a paper-thin blue blanket. Except for the bars, the other walls were bare concrete. "Where am I?" she asked.

The guard popped his gum and laughed. "The Hilton, where else?" Still laughing, he turned and strolled away.

Harley rubbed her eyes. She felt tired, and her mouth was as dry as the desert. She reached out and touched one of the cold metal bars. Wherever she was, it was obvious that Harley wasn't in the backseat of Detective Locke's car anymore. Someone had to have taken her out of the car, brought her inside, and put her on the bunk. The idea that she could have slept through all of that bothered her a lot.

Harley heard a clang and a rattle from the far end of the hallway, followed by the sharp sound of footfalls on the tiled floor. Detective Locke stepped in front of Harley's cell.

"Are you finished with your nap?" he asked.

Harley shrugged. "I guess so. How did I get up here?"

Locke leaned against the bars. "You conked out in my car. We tried everything to wake you up, even had a doctor in to look at you." He shook his head. "It's a good thing you woke up. We were about to transfer you to the hospital."

"Maybe I should have stayed asleep." Harley turned away from the detective and stared at the concrete wall. "At least I would have been out of here until you hauled me back.

"Oh, I don't think you have to worry about that," said the detective. He put his hand around the bars and pulled. The whole front of the cell slid to the side. "You're free to go whenever you're ready."

Harley stared at the open door in surprise. "Did I sleep through a whole jail term?"

Locke gave her a thin smile. "Not quite. It seems you have some friends in high places, Ms. Vincent. Lawyers have been arguing on your behalf all morning, and we've even had a call from the mayor's office."

"For me?" Harley was beginning to wonder if she was still asleep. The idea that someone from the mayor's office would call about her seemed like the wildest kind of dream.

"You seem to be a very popular young lady." Locke's smile disappeared. "I want you to understand that this doesn't mean you've been cleared. You're still under investigation. Got that?"

"Yeah," Harley replied with a nod.

The detective gestured at the hallway. "If you'll come with me, I need you to sign a couple of papers so we can get you out of here."

Still dazed, Harley got up and followed Locke down the hallway. He led her into a room that smelled heavily of double-strength coffee and old cigarette smoke. Harley sat down at a battered metal desk and accepted a pair of release forms that Locke slid toward her. Only as she was signing the papers did she figure out who her strange benefactor had to be.

"Cain," she whispered.

Detective Locke raised an eyebrow. "What was that?"

Harley shook her head and pushed the forms back to the detective. "Nothing." Cain's claim to be an FBI agent had been a lie, but Harley had seen again and again that Cain and his organization had agents everywhere. If anyone was helping her, it had to be Cain.

Locke took the documents that Harley had signed and slipped them into an envelope. "All right," he said. "I have one more item for you." The detective reached into the inside pocket of his trench coat and pulled out the cylinder of artificial blood. "I believe this is yours. It's not even flammable, so it couldn't have been used in the fire. It's chemical composition is something like liquid Teflon, but it's certainly not a controlled substance, so we had no reason to impound it."

Harley took it eagerly. "Thanks," she said. She was relieved that the police had used very little of the fluid in their testing. The cylinder was nearly full.

"Just remember that what I said about leaving town still applies," commanded Locke. "If I have to fish you out of the train station again, it'll take more than a phone call from His Honor to get you sprung."

"Right." Harley looked around the squad room, almost expecting to see Cain looking back at her from some corner. "Tell me something, Detective Locke. These people that came to get me out, did you see a man with them? A tall man with a hat like yours?"

Locke frowned and shook his head. "Nope, doesn't ring a bell. I only saw the lawyer." He stood and held out his hand. "Stay nearby, Ms. Vincent."

Harley nodded and shook the detective's hand. "Don't worry," she said. "I don't have anywhere to go."

She started across the room and was almost out the door when Locke called her name. "What is it?" she asked.

The detective stepped toward her. "I just remembered that someone else showed up here asking about you. A young woman came in twice."

Harley smiled. It had to be Dee. Everything was starting to make sense after all. Dee, Cain, and Scott must all be working together to get her out. Scott might even have tapped some of Kenyon's millions to pay for the sudden appearance of a lawyer.

"Let me guess," said Harley. "This young woman who came to look for me, was she short with auburn hair and kind of a round face?"

Detective Locke shook his head. "Nope, not even close. This woman was tall, with black hair and dark eyes. Very striking."

Harley shook her head slowly. "I can't think of anyone like that."

Detective Locke rubbed at his square chin. "Funny," he said. "Because my first thought was that you must be related."

"What?"

Lock shrugged. "This girl looked enough like you to be your sister."

SEVEN

The sun was already getting close to the horizon by the time Kenyon Moor reached the base of the arch.

High above him, the gleaming metal of the monument caught and held the fading light of the sun. From far away, it had been hard to get an idea of the scale of the thing. Close up, it was enormous. Kenyon's parents had owned a very large construction company, and he had been involved with architecture projects all his life, but the arch still looked impossible. If he had seen the plans for such a building in his father's office, he would have sworn it couldn't be built.

For the tenth time, Kenyon pulled the slip of paper from his pocket. In the fading light he had to squint to read the handwriting. He could just manage to read it.

ARCH—SOUTH LEG
7 P.M.

He was in the right place, and it was almost the right time. Now all he had to do was wait until the mystery woman made her appearance.

All afternoon he had been thinking of the way she had battled the shadow man. It had been a display of incredible skill and power that far exceeded anything Kenyon had ever seen before. He wondered how long it had taken her to acquire such command—and if she would train him to use the same techniques.

His wait in the park turned out to be very short. Only a minute after he took up a position beside the south leg of the vast arch, he spotted a figure jogging down one of the curving, tree-lined walkways. As the figure drew closer, he realized it was the woman he was waiting for.

She had changed out of the loose black clothes she had worn earlier in the day. Now she was dressed in a simple white T-shirt and running shorts. Her braided hair bounced against her back with each step, and her long tan legs stretched out in a smooth gait. Watching her run, Kenyon had a sudden clear memory of Harley. For the first time, he realized that this woman looked a lot like Harley. She had the same hair, the same smooth olive skin. In fact, they looked so similar he was surprised he hadn't noted the resemblance right away.

Kenyon raised his hand in greeting as the woman approached.

The running woman glanced at him for only a moment. "Come on," she said as she passed him. She kept on running without missing a stride.

Kenyon stared after her in surprise for a moment, then hurried to catch up. He had to sprint to make up the distance. Even when he was running at her side, Kenyon found the woman's pace more than a little difficult. "Can we stop?" he asked between breaths.

The woman shook her head. "No."

"Why not?"

"There are prying ears and eyes everywhere, Mr. Moor." She waved an arm in a gesture that took in the whole park. "Even here there are bound to be some that would love to hear our little conversation. If we're to avoid them, we'll have to stay on the move."

Kenyon didn't reply—he was too busy breathing. Both Harley and Noah had been on the track team, and Kenyon was sure either of them would have handled the woman's pace without a problem. But running was definitely not Kenyon's favorite activity. He liked to think he was in good shape, but after going no more than halfway around the park, Kenyon was ready to drop.

The walkway ended at a long sweeping stair that curved down to the riverfront where dozens of old-fashioned steamboats lined up to offer everything from gambling to fast food. Kenyon hoped the woman would stop at the stairs, but she charged right down the steps without pausing. He struggled to keep up, but his legs were beginning to feel like wet noodles. Halfway down, he stumbled, missed a step, and fell, bruising his knees. Finally, Kenyon's fatigue overcame his desire to impress this strange woman.

"Hey!" he called as he climbed to his feet. "Can we at least slow down a little?"

The woman slowed her pace and dropped back to his side. "Just keep moving," she ordered.

Running along beside her, Kenyon could see the way the smooth muscles worked in the woman's long, tan legs, and the sweat-damp strands of hair that pulled free from her braid to crowd around her face. She seemed almost impossibly fit—and terribly attractive.

He felt a stab of guilt. Harley had been dead less than a day, and already he was thinking of someone new. Only a few hours ago, he had been thinking about how much he had loved Harley. He had never admitted his feelings, but they had been real.

"Who are you?" he asked the woman.

"My name is Selena," she replied. She glanced over at him for a moment. "And you are Kenyon Moor."

Kenyon shook his head. "How do you know my name?"

Selena's lips curved in a slight smile. "It should be obvious by now that I know a lot more than your name. The organization I work for has been very interested in you, Kenyon."

Kenyon stopped in his tracks. "Organization?" His head swam, and he felt the blanket of his anger rising over him. "I should have known."

Selena stopped and turned back toward him. "What's wrong?"

"Tell me," Kenyon replied. "Do you work for

Umbra, or is it Unit 17? Or is it this unnamed thing that Cain works for?"

"It's not like that," Selena said, shaking her head. "Our organization works against all those groups."

Kenyon gave a bitter laugh. "Sure, I've heard that before. You want to knock off all the others so you can grab everything for yourselves."

"It's not that way." Selena pushed damp hair away from her face. "Look, you lost your parents last year. From what we've been able to put together, Unit 17 was behind their deaths."

"Am I supposed to trust you because you know that fact?" Kenyon folded his arms across his chest. "For all I know, you're *from* Unit 17."

"I didn't tell you that to gain your trust," said Selena. She cocked her head to the side and swept her dark gaze over Kenyon. "This is a war, Kenyon. Just because it's fought in secret doesn't mean there aren't casualties."

"My parents never signed up for a war," Kenyon shot back.

"Neither did mine." Selena pointed toward the river. "They died right out there, along with my sister and a dozen other members of my family. They died when the group called Legion decided they had become a threat."

Kenyon drew in a deep breath. "Legion?" His own dealings with the group had been brief, but he had no doubt they were capable of cruelties as great as anything done by Unit 17. "Why would Legion kill your family?"

Selena stared across the flowing brown waters of the river. "For years, my father was interested in the idea of paranormal abilities. If they had been poor, people might have even said he was crazy on the subject." She shrugged. "But our family was wealthy, and my father's interests were viewed as just another eccentricity."

Kenyon took a step closer. Despite his earlier distrust, the woman's story captured his attention. "Did your father discover the secret groups?"

"No," Selena replied. "He didn't know they existed. He funded a research center on the paranormal at Washington University. At first, they got very few results, but a few years ago, they began to achieve spectacular success. It seemed that they were on the brink of proving the existence of the paranormal. They were about to become famous." Selena paused in her story and shook her head slowly. "Only that's not how it turned out."

"What happened?" asked Kenyon.

"Just days before they were going to announce their discovery, the national papers published a series of articles saying that everything the foundation had discovered was faked." Selena's eyes narrowed as she recalled the story, and Kenyon saw the muscles in her shoulders tighten. "They made my father into a laughingstock."

"It was the secret groups, wasn't it?" Kenyon asked.

Selena nodded. "The publicity was so bad that

the university pulled the plug on the whole project." She gave a short, humorless laugh. "But that didn't stop my father. He turned around and set up a private foundation. They made great, successful strides. And then they decided to hold this big press conference, so my father . . . my father chartered a steamship." She stopped again and stood there facing the water.

The eastern sky had turned a deep purple, and a chill breeze whistled along the river valley. From down by the line of boats, Kenyon heard the laughter of people walking in and out of the floating casinos.

"Maybe we should start moving again," Kenyon suggested softly.

Selena nodded. "We should, but only after I finish this story." She tossed her head back and stood with her face to the darkening sky. "My father chartered a historic steamship, hired a band, had the whole thing catered. He was going to do it up right. It was going to be an event, not just a press conference." She raised her hand and pointed out beyond the row of docked boats. "They were right out there, in the center of the river, when the ship's boilers blew. Almost fifty people lost their lives, including everyone in my family." Her dark eyes closed shut against the memory. "The only reason I wasn't out there with them is because I had the flu."

Kenyon looked out at the swirling water of the river. His own parents had died in a mysterious air crash. He had spent every day since then trying to exact revenge for their deaths, but he had never gone to the scene of the accident. "How do you know it was Legion?" he asked.

"That's when the organization stepped in," Selena replied. "After my parents were gone, they got in touch with me." She turned and looked at Kenyon. "I said before that you weren't the only one who had suffered a tragedy because of the *Cunnart.*"

"The what?"

"*Cunnart,*" Selena repeated. "It's an old Celtic term. It means *danger,* or *dangerous.* We use it to apply to all of the secret groups."

"Who is we?" asked Kenyon.

A group of chattering tourists approached down the long staircase and started walking toward them. "Come on," said Selena. "We should go." She turned and began running down the street.

Kenyon sprinted a few steps and fell in at her side. "Who is this group you belong to?"

Selena didn't answer for a moment. "A lot of people have lost their friends and family to the *Cunnart,*" she said at last. "Some of the groups formed thousands of years in the past. Their hands are stained with the blood of millions."

"And you oppose them?" asked Kenyon between breaths.

She nodded. "That's right. Our group has only one goal—the complete eradication of the *Cunnart.*"

Kenyon felt a wave of emotion that was part joy,

part raw-red anger. The destruction of the secret groups had been his own private goal from the moment of his parent's death. The other allies he had found: Scott, Cain, even Harley—had also had their own agendas. Harley wanted to find Noah and her father. Scott was endlessly searching for his foster sister, Chloe. Cain was only out for himself. Now Kenyon had found his perfect partner.

"I want to join you," he said in a rush. "I want to see Unit 17 and Umbra and all the others ripped out of hiding and torn apart."

Selena looked over at him with a broad smile. "We thought you were a good candidate. Come on, follow me." She put on a burst of speed as they reached the end of the sidewalk and turned up a slope. Kenyon had to run for all he was worth just to stay close to her.

They reached the entrance to a multistory parking garage. To Kenyon's surprise, Selena dashed around the gate and into the dimly lit parking lot beyond. He dodged a car and followed her. They ran together up a sharply curving ramp and out into a level of the garage that was completely empty. There Selena came to an abrupt halt.

"We should be safe here for a few minutes," she said.

Kenyon bent over and put his hands on his knees as he tried to recover from the hard run. "What happens now?" he asked. "Is there some kind of initiation?"

"We don't have time for games," said Selena. She looked into Kenyon's face, her dark eyes glittering in the dim light. "We want to put you to work, right away, destroying those who killed your parents and your friend Harley."

Again Kenyon felt a savage, overwhelming mixture of joy and rage. "Yes," he replied eagerly. "Yes, that's what I want, too."

"Good." From some hidden place in her snug clothing, Selena produced something small and flat. "Here," she said. "Take this."

Kenyon held out his hand and accepted the tiny device. It was barely bigger than a matchbook, with a tiny nozzlelike opening at one end and a pair of buttons at the other. For its size, it was surprisingly heavy. "What is this?" he asked.

"A weapon," Selena answered. "We've developed it for use against the *Cunnart* and their agents. You'll find it's a lot more powerful than you might think from its size."

Kenyon closed his hand around the tiny gun. "Will you teach me to fight the way you do?"

Selena nodded. "That, and more. We'll teach you everything you need." She stepped closer to Kenyon, so close that he could smell the tangy, salty scent left by her run and see the tiny drops of sweat that beaded her forehead. "Come with me," she said. "I'll see that you get a chance to use that weapon very soon."

"That's good," Kenyon replied. He found

himself unable to look away from Selena's large, dark eyes. "This group I'm joining, does it have a name?"

"Oh, yes." Selena bent her face close to his and dropped her voice to a whisper that was at once soft and fierce. "We call ourselves Vengeance."

A night of fire and a day of rain had reduced the Washington Avenue Book Emporium to a grimy hole in the street between its newer, shinier neighbors.

Harley stood on the sidewalk just outside the fluttering barrier of yellow police tape and looked in at the damp mass of bricks. She had taken the tiny amount of cash she had meant to spend on a train ticket and instead purchased a light jacket, a cheap canvas book bag, and a couple of burgers. Now she had a place to store the tube of artificial blood, and the rumble in her stomach was gone, but she still had no plan for what to do next.

She looked at the ruin of the bookstore and shook her head. A day ago, she thought. Can it really be a day ago that Kenyon and I went into the store?

Noah had said that time was funny inside the sphere—fast sometimes and sometimes slow. Harley felt as though her whole life worked that way. Months would go by in a kind of dreamy daze, during which nothing much happened and even less was remembered. Then a period of hours would hold more terror, more tragedy, and more emotion than any normal year.

Harley closed her eyes. She wanted to talk to

Noah again. She wanted to know what he had meant about something being wrong with her father, and to learn more about life inside the sphere. Most of all, she wanted to join him again in the tranquil village at the side of the woods, with its green fields and stands of wildflowers. After what had happened in St. Louis, Harley felt as though she were ready to move to that village—permanently.

She felt a light touch on her shoulder.

Harley spun around, ready to face the police, a shadow man, or anything else the secret organizations might throw her way. What she found was a surprise.

"Harley?" asked a tentative voice. "Is that you?"

Harley found herself looking down at a pair of thick glasses perched on an upturned nose and a round face framed by auburn hair. "Dee?" Harley breathed. She grabbed the smaller girl and wrapped her in a tight hug. "Dee! I was so worried about you."

Dee laughed. "You were worried about *me!* The last thing we knew, you were captured by the bad guys. We thought you were dead."

Harley released Dee and stepped back. She looked down at Dee's face and smiled. "No, I'm fine. You saved me. How did you ever manage to break into Mr. Antolin's computer system?"

Dee returned her smile. "That's cool," she said. "You'll have to let Scott tell you how we pulled it off." She gestured to her left.

Harley turned her head and saw tall, gangly Scott

standing at the edge of the road. A dark windbreaker covered his thin frame and his blond ponytail hung down below his shoulders. His features were split by a grin.

"Hi, Harley," he said shyly.

"Hi, nothing." Harley ran to him and hugged him as tight as she could. "Thank you," she said.

Scott returned her hug for a moment, then backed away. Though it was dark, Harley was willing to bet he was flushing with embarrassment. "It wasn't really very hard to get into the computers," he said modestly. "We had a lock on your position from the handheld unit you were carrying. Then we noticed a high level of CPDP activity in your area. The packet code was a variant of DES, which is pretty tough, but we were able to put a forty-chip multitasking unit on the job. After that, it was just a matter of—"

Harley laughed and held up her hands. "Don't try to explain any more, you've lost me already." She stepped back from them both and shook her head. She smiled so hard her face hurt. "You two are amazing."

"We're awfully glad to see you," said Scott. "All the way out here, Dee kept saying you'd be all right, but I was really worried."

"I'm okay," said Harley, her voice dropping to a whisper. She looked down at her singed and tattered clothing. "I've been cleaner, but I'm fine."

Dee folded her arms and nodded. "See," she said

in a satisfied tone. "When are you going to learn you should always listen to me?"

Scott craned his long neck. "So, where's Kenyon?"

The smile froze on Harley's face. "Kenyon," she repeated.

"Yeah," said Scott. "I know he's going to be mad at us for losing Cain and for leaving the mansion, but when we lost contact I really thought we should get out here as soon as possible. So," he said nervously, "you think he'll be mad?"

Harley swallowed hard. "No . . . I mean, I don't . . ." She stopped, took a deep breath, and looked back and forth between Scott and Dee. "What I mean is, Kenyon didn't make it."

Dee's eyes widened behind the rim of her glasses. "What do you mean he didn't make it?"

"There was a fire." Harley gestured helplessly toward the ruins of the bookstore. Tears welled in her eyes, and her throat grew tight as she tried to find the words to explain Kenyon's death. "We were trapped in underground tunnels. There was a fire. And Kenyon—he didn't get out."

Scott looked as if someone had punched him in the stomach. His long frame bent almost double and he staggered back. "He can't be dead," he whispered.

"You don't know what it was like down there," Harley said in a hushed voice. For the first time since she escaped from the basement, she found herself really crying. Tears rolled in steady trickles down her cheeks. "There was fire everywhere. It was like being caught in a slow explosion."

Scott's thin face hardened and he shook his head. "But you didn't actually see him die, did you? You didn't see his body."

"No," Harley agreed. "But—"

"He's not dead," Scott declared firmly. He stepped past Harley and walked straight into the barricade of police tape. The plastic tape stretched and broke around him, leaving streamers of yellow flapping from Scott's shoulders as he hurried toward the smoldering pit.

"Scott, wait!" Harley called. She wiped the tears away from her face. "The police have been searching in there all day. There's nothing more to be found."

Scott ignored her. He reached the edge of the tumble of bricks and began to climb downward.

Dee sighed. "Come on," she said. "We'd better get him." She ran through the opening that Scott had made in the barrier and stood above him on the rubble pile. "Get out of there!" she called down.

He glanced up for a moment, his face pale in the light from the surrounding street lamps. "But Kenyon—"

"Is gone," Dee interrupted, "and if you climb down into that mess, you'll probably break your neck. Then we'll have two dead."

Scott paused, but his eyes were still turned toward the damp bricks and the lake of ash-stained water at the center of the pit. "He can't be dead," he said so softly that Harley could barely make out the words.

"Maybe he's not," said Dee. "But you're not going to find anything messing around down there in the dark. Come out of there, and we'll go somewhere we can all talk."

For a moment, Scott didn't reply. A small avalanche of bricks broke loose from the pile at his feet and tumbled down to splash into the water. "All right," he said finally. He turned and climbed back up the slope.

Dee stepped through the broken tape and pointed down the road. "Come on," she said to Harley. "We've got a van waiting down there."

Harley followed them to a dark blue full-sized van parked along the road. Dee climbed into the driver's seat. Scott opened the seat on the passenger side, but instead of getting in, he waved Harley toward the open chair. "You better take this place," he said. "I've got some stuff in the back."

"All right." Harley slipped off her book bag and held it in her lap as she climbed inside. Scott went through the sliding door behind her and took a place in the back. Harley turned around to look.

The "stuff" that Scott had mentioned was actually an incredible array of gear. Most of the seats in the van had been removed, leaving two chairs on swiveling mounts. On either side of these chairs were a pair of computer terminals and an incomprehensible array of electronic equipment. Further back were a group of yellow plastic boxes and bundles held together with buckled straps.

Scott slipped into the front chair and pulled the door shut. His shoulders slumped as he looked at Harley. "Are you sure he's dead?" he asked softly.

Harley pressed her lips together and nodded. "The last time I saw Kenyon, he was still partially strapped down to a table. Then there was an explosion, and I lost him. After that, the fire grew so quickly, I barely made it out. I don't see any way he could have escaped."

From the expression on Scott's face, Harley could tell he still wasn't prepared to accept the death of his friend. "Maybe," he said after a moment, "but as long as you didn't actually *see* a body, there's still a chance."

"Yes," Harley admitted, "there's always a chance."

Dee started the van and began to drive west along a boulevard lined with trees and huge, brooding old homes. "I think it's time we have an information exchange," she said. "We need to know everything we can about what happened to you and Kenyon, and we'll explain what happened with us."

"That sounds like an idea," Harley agreed. She started to explain what had gone on in the basement of the bookstore, but her throat still felt raw. "You go first," she suggested.

Dee nodded. She was quiet for a moment. The reflected light from the van's headlights shone on her glasses, and despite Dee's calm behavior, Harley could see that she had also been crying.

"Here's what happened in Stone Harbor," Dee began. "After you and Kenyon left, we had two jobs: take care of Cain and feed you any information you needed. For the first couple of hours, Cain was no problem. He was so short of the stuff he used for blood that he lay there like he was dead. A couple of times, I even thought he *was* dead. Then Scott started checking into finding more of the fake blood."

Scott leaned forward in his chair. "It was an oxygenated fluorine and resin compound, kind of like Teflon," he added.

"I think I found some of it," said Harley. She flipped open the top of her book bag, reached inside, and came out with the tube of greenish fluid. "I think this is the stuff."

Scott took the tube from her and tilted it back and forth. "This looks right," he said. "There's no way to be sure without doing some analysis."

"Yeah," continued Dee. "Anyway, we didn't have any of the real thing, so Scott started checking the database and found something very similar that—"

"It had a different resin makeup," said Scott. "But the oxygenation ratio was almost exactly the same."

Dee stopped the van and turned around in her seat. "Let me tell it, okay?"

Scott nodded.

"Okay, cool." Dee started the van again and

continued down the street. "Well, to make it short, we found some of the stuff. We had to pay a chemical supply company about half the money in Kenyon's bank account to get a liter of the goop flown up to Stone Harbor. Then once we got it, we were afraid to use it. I mean, it was one thing to buy the stuff, it was another to shove it into the veins of a guy who's lying there unconscious."

"I can understand that," Harley said. "So what did you do?"

Dee shrugged and turned right onto a road that wound along the edge of a large park. "Nothing," she replied. "We tried putting a little bit of it into him, and we couldn't see any change. We got scared to do any more and just left the rest of the stuff and the transfusion equipment sitting next to Cain's bed." They reached a stop sign, and Dee turned to look at Harley. "We left him alone for a few minutes, and the next thing we knew, Cain, the equipment, and the bottle of expensive goop were gone."

Harley nodded. "And then?"

"That's pretty much it," said Dee. "We figured out where you where, broke into the computer, and then decided we had better come and get you."

Harley thought for a moment. "Things have been pretty strange on my end." Briefly she explained all the things that had happened to her and Kenyon: the car chase in Washington, the killer who had stalked them on a train in St. Louis, their capture by the huge Mr. Antolin.

"Right up until the end, I thought it was Tessera, or maybe Unit 17 that was behind everything," Harley concluded. "It wasn't until the last second that I found out who was really behind it."

"Let me guess," said Dee. "It's Billie."

Harley gaped at her friend in surprise. "How did you know?"

"I didn't," replied Dee. "I just figure that everything that's going on is Billie's fault. So far, it seems to work."

"Well, it works in this case," Harley agreed. "Billie's been behind this thing from the beginning. She's the one that's been causing the fracture in Cain's group. She sent the killers after me. She did it all."

Scott leaned forward from his place in the rear of the van. "Was it Billie who killed Kenyon?"

"She didn't do it herself," Harley said, "but she was the real cause behind what happened."

"Then we have to do something," said Scott through clenched teeth. "We have to stop her."

Harley was surprised at the anger she heard in Scott's voice. During everything that had happened before, Scott had been the one person that always keep his good nature and his sense of humor.

Dee pulled the van over to the side of the road and stopped. "Some of this equipment might be able to find Billie."

Scott nodded in agreement. "If she's anywhere nearby, I think we can spot her."

Harley thought about the idea. Billie had survived the collapse of Umbra headquarters and enough injuries to kill a dozen normal people. If they found her, it might be the death of them all. But if they didn't find her, Billie would be free to continue her schemes.

"All right," Harley said at last. "You find her and I'll stop her."

"How?" asked Scott.

"There's only one way to stop someone like Billie," Harley said firmly. She drew a deep breath. "Once we find her, I'll kill her."

Even to someone whose family had constructed skyscrapers around the world, the lobby of the Riverside Building was impressive.

Kenyon peered up at the roof arching almost a hundred feet over his head. Everything was covered in creamy Italian marble and polished gray diorite. Even the outside of the building was sheathed in slabs of Icelandic granite that went all the way to the roof. He couldn't begin to imagine the expense of such a construction.

"Nice place," Kenyon said as he followed Selena across the vast, vaulted lobby.

She glanced at him over her shoulder and smiled. "Like it? My father used to keep his offices in this building. After he died, I took over the top two floors."

Kenyon nodded. Selena's story sounded much like his own. He followed her to an elevator set in the corner that was marked simply Atrium. The door opened at their approach. Once inside, he noticed there were no buttons. In fact, there were no controls of any kind. A few seconds later, the elevator doors closed and the car began to ascend with astounding speed.

When the doors opened again, Kenyon could barely believe what he saw.

Leading out of the elevator was a path made from rounded river cobbles and patches of pale sand. To either side were fields of swaying grass, backed by clusters of trees. In the distance the trees grew taller and tighter, forming the edge of a deep green forest.

"Well," said Selena. "What do you think?"

Kenyon could only stand and shake his head. "Wow," he said softly. "I've never seen anything like this. It's wonderful."

Selena smiled. "Thanks. It's home."

She stepped out of the elevator and walked along the curving path. Kenyon followed her between low shrubs and into the deeper trees. A flight of birds burst from a thicket on the right and went circling up under the high, peaked glass ceiling. As far as Kenyon could tell, the entire penthouse of the building had been turned into a forest the size of a city block. The mixture of trees and shrubs looked southern to Kenyon, almost tropical. If he ignored the glass walls that bounded the space on all sides, he might have believed that he was standing in a field somewhere in Florida, or maybe Central America.

A brook crossed the path, and Kenyon found himself splashing through ankle-deep water. On the other side, a copse of trees stood in the middle of a field of waist-high grass. Selena left the stone path and led Kenyon through the grass to a gap in the ring of trees. Beyond the trees was another surprise—a computer workstation and a pair of chairs.

Selena dropped into one of the padded chairs. She smiled up at Kenyon. "I find this a very relaxing place to do my work," she said. "Please, have a seat."

Kenyon sat down gratefully. Only once he was sitting did he realize how tired he was. It seemed as though he had been on his feet, constantly on the move, for at least three days. "What happens now?" he asked.

"Now we plan." Selena leaned back in her chair and templed her fingers together in front of her face. "Now we prepare."

"To move against Cain," said Kenyon.

Selena nodded. "Exactly. First, let's hear what Cain told you."

"He showed up looking like he was dying," said Kenyon. "He told us that a splinter group called Tessera had formed in his organization and that this group was trying to kill him."

"That fits well with the information we've uncovered." Selena raised her long legs and folded them under herself in the chair. "The Tessera idea was discussed in Cain's transmissions as the best way to engage your friend Harley. It was felt that she would hurry to defend anyone she viewed as a friend."

Kenyon nodded. "She would. Harley is . . ." He paused and looked away. "Harley was like that."

"By all accounts, she was exceptional," said Selena. "She and her friend Noah did an incredible amount of damage to Unit 17, Umbra, and Legion. I would say they've done more to help our cause than any other two individuals in the world."

"So why didn't you invite *them* into your organization?" asked Kenyon.

"We might have, but we weren't sure of their motives. Harley's father worked with Unit 17, and Noah was directly involved with Legion. We weren't sure we could trust them."

Kenyon's jaw tightened. "You could trust Harley."

"Of course," Selena said with a nod. "We can see that now. It's too bad we were so slow reaching our decision."

"So what about Cain?" asked Kenyon.

Selena stood up. "We will kill him, of course." She reached around behind her back and worked her fingers in her braided hair. The thick strands fell loose and swept forward around her face in a heavy black curtain. Loose, her hair dangled over her shoulder and down her back almost to her waist. "But if we were to run out and try to kill Cain right now, we'd soon find ourselves just as dead as the thousands of others who have found themselves killed by Cain's nameless organization."

A weariness fell over Kenyon. He looked up at Selena's calm oval face with her extraordinary dark eyes, and felt a wave of emotion too tangled to ever sort out. "How do we get ready?" he asked.

Selena stepped toward him. "We work together. I have all the resources of Vengeance behind me. We use them to track Cain's every movement. And, if possible, we might even be able to stay one jump ahead."

"How?"

"Remember, Cain is only one member of a greater organization. He may have planned the execution of your friend, but he made those plans on the orders of others." Selena leaned down, the heavy curtain of her hair brushing against Kenyon's cheek. "If we're very lucky, we may catch Cain together with other members of his killer organization. With one blow, we might be able to deliver the same kind of damage that Harley did to Umbra."

Kenyon nodded slowly. "That would be . . ." He tried to think of the right word, but his mind swam. Where the strands of Selena's hair touched his cheek, his skin seemed hypersensitive. He could feel every separate strand as if it were wired straight into his nervous system. "That would . . ."

Selena placed her hands on the arms of Kenyon's chair and lowered her face until it was only an inch from his. "We'll work together," she whispered.

Kenyon nodded. "Yes."

"And together, we can accomplish what no one could ever do alone—we can destroy them all."

"Destroy them," repeated Kenyon.

Selena brought her lips to his. At her kiss Kenyon felt a burst of intensely pleasurable energy swarm through his body. He reached out and wrapped his arms around Selena, pulling her against him.

Kenyon felt a moment of confusion that bordered on panic. He started to say something about Harley. He started to tell Selena to stop. Then all words—all thoughts—were erased from Kenyon's mind. Instead he found himself overwhelmed by feelings of rage, mixed with desire, stirred with a passion he had never known. Selena's body was warm in his arms. Despite her obvious strength, her skin was very soft under his hands. Soft and warm. Her lips pressed against his with ruthless enthusiasm. Her hair fell across his face like waves of flame.

A red haze rose up in Kenyon mind. His arms pulled Selena ever tighter. The cords in his neck grew tight. He pulled his face away from Selena's and cried out in pure fury as his rage rose to a peak. Then everything went dark.

Sometime later, Kenyon opened his eyes and found himself sitting on one of the padded chairs in the shadowed interior of the rooftop forest. Something blacker than the night shifted nearby, and Kenyon heard a deep rumbling growl. He started to sit up, but a hand pressed gently against his chest.

"Rest," Selena said softly. "You must be ready tomorrow."

A shadow of the anger he had felt crossed Kenyon's mind. "Cain," he said, his voice was dry and hoarse. "What about Cain?"

Selena knelt beside his chair and brought her lips close to his ear. "Don't worry about Cain," she said. "We'll have no trouble finding him."

"Why not?"

"Because," she whispered, "he is coming to us."

TEN

"Harley?"

Harley moaned, turned over, and pulled the blanket around her shoulders. Surely it was way too early for school. She had only been asleep for seconds, minutes at the most.

"Harley, we're getting a reading on Scott's equipment."

The words took a moment to sink in. When she opened her eyes, Harley found she was lying curled on the floor in the back of the van. She sat up and rubbed her eyes. Dee was looking down at her from the rear of the two swiveling chairs. In the front chair, Scott leaned over what looked like a disorganized mass of circuit boards and wire.

"What have you found?" Harley asked.

Scott looked up and shrugged. "It's hard to tell," he said. "Here, come take a look for yourself."

Harley stood up and squeezed past Dee's chair to stand beside Scott. On the workbench in front of him, a metal frame held a trio of circuit boards. Portions of the boards had the neat, square look of factory designs, but in other places the boards were spotted with blobs of gray solder and loops of colored wire. Attached to one side of the circuit boards was a small box decorated with three unmarked knobs. On the other side was an aging black-and-white computer monitor.

"What is this thing for?" she asked.

Scott slowly twisted one of the three knobs. "It's a little hard to explain," he said. "It detects energy waves that operate on a frequency way above radio, or even microwave."

Harley nodded. "I can understand that much. Where do these high frequency waves come from?"

"From your head," Scott replied.

"What?"

Scott gave the dials another fine adjustment. "Not just your head, almost any head. I think this type of energy generates when the brain is solving certain types of problems. I think we can use this energy to find Billie."

"I don't get it," Harley said. "If everybody generates this kind of energy, then how do we use it to find Billie?"

"Easy," Scott relied. "Almost everybody generates some measurable amount of these waves, but certain people generate a lot more." He tapped his finger against the display screen. "All these sparks represent sources of this energy."

Harley studied the display screen. To her, it looked like some kind of static, or maybe a computerized image of an anthill. Streams of white points moved along in lines, while others were sprayed across the screen. The points flickered, popping in and out of existence. In the center of the screen was a white smudge that pulsated and changed from a pinpoint to a thumb-sized glow and back again.

"All these spots are people?" she asked.

Scott nodded. "They produce this energy for a few seconds, then stop."

"Why?"

"I don't know," he replied with a shrug. "I don't really understand where this stuff comes from at all."

Harley studied the fluttering streams of sparks. It was strange, and a little creepy, to think that those points of light were measuring something that was radiating from people's skulls. She pointed to the pulsing point in the center of the screen. "What about this spot in the middle?"

"Oh," replied Scott. "That bright spot is you."

"What?" Harley backed away from the screen and looked at Scott in surprise. "How can that be me?"

"Like I said, some people produce more of this energy than others. You're one. Cain is another." Scott bent down, his ponytail swinging around his shoulders, and came up with a piece of paper lined with squiggles of ink. "That was how I detected this energy in the first place. When you and Cain were both in the mansion, something interfered with the most sensitive electronics. I was able to trace it to these high frequency spikes." He held out the strip of paper and ran his finger along the line. "I started working on a way to measure this while you were gone. Right here, where the line levels out, that's where Cain disappeared."

Harley studied the tracing for a moment, but it made even less sense than the sparks flying across the display screen. "So Cain and I both put out a lot of this energy."

"Right," said Scott. "We were able to use this equipment to locate you by the bookstore. And I think other exceptional people might also produce large amounts."

"There's nothing exceptional about me," Harley said quickly. "I'm just a regular person."

Scott looked up at her, his blue eyes more serious than she had ever seen before. "If you say so," he replied. "But the instruments don't agree. The level of this energy that you're producing is at least a hundred times greater than the average person."

Harley looked at the pulsing light at the center of the display screen. From me? she thought. It seemed impossible that she had some kind of power normal people didn't. Unit 17 had thought that both Harley and her mother had special abilities, and there was her strange connection to Noah, but she still had a hard time thinking of herself as someone with paranormal powers.

"It makes me feel like some kind of freak," Harley said.

"Maybe you can get in the special class at school," Dee called from the back of the van.

"Very funny."

Dee shrugged. "Just trying to be helpful."

Harley gave her friend the best glare she could manage, then turned back to the display. "So how is this thing going to help us find Billie?"

Scott reached out and twisted one of the dials at the side of the makeshift device. As he did, the cluster of blinking sparks grew tighter. Very few new points appeared around the edge of the screen as the image expanded, leaving a wide border of darkness.

"The power falls off quickly with distance," said Scott. "Part of the reason your spot looks so bright is because you're right on top of the equipment. When I expand the range, normal people don't make enough energy to be seen at all."

"So what are we looking for?" asked Harley.

"Hang on a second. . . .There." Scott tapped his finger against the glass. In one corner of the screen a bright point of light appeared for a few seconds, faded, and disappeared. "Whoever's generating that source," said Scott, "is putting out about half of what you do, but about fifty times as much as normal."

Normal, Harley thought. I'm not normal. "You think it could be Billie?"

"I don't know," said Scott. "But I think it's worth checking out."

On the screen the point of light pulsed again. "All right," Harley agreed. "Let's go see who's sending up a flare." She pushed open the side door of the van, and started to get out, but waiting on the sidewalk was a tall figure with a camel's hair suit and a fedora perched on his head.

"Good morning, Ms. Vincent," said Detective Locke. "I see you located some friends."

Harley blinked in surprise. "How did you find me?"

"We got a tip that you were trying to leave town again. Our tipster was nice enough to include a license plate and description of this van." The detective peered through the open door at Scott and the array of gadgets behind him. "What's your name, son?"

"Scott Handleson."

"Is this vehicle yours?"

Scott shook his head. "It belongs to a friend."

"I see," said Locke. "What about identification, do you have any of that?"

"Sure." Scott got up from his seat and unfolded his tall frame as he stepped from the van. He dug into the pocket of his jeans and pulled out a wallet.

"Hold it right there," called a voice from the back of the van.

Dee Janes emerged, her glasses flashing in the morning sun. "Don't show him your ID," she said firmly. "He's got no reason to see it."

Locke turned to look down at Dee. "Who have we here? An aspiring young lawyer?"

Dee hopped from the van and folded her arms. "We haven't done anything wrong," she insisted. "You've got no reason to stop us."

Locke's dark eyes were hard as flint. "Your friend Ms. Vincent is being investigated for arson and possible murder."

"Is she?" Dee pressed her glasses up her nose and peered up at the detective. "And has she been charged with anything?"

Detective Locke frowned. "Not at this time."

Dee smiled. "Cool," she said. "Then there's no problem associating with her, is there?"

Harley could see the muscles in the detective's jaw tighten. "No," he replied. "There isn't."

"Then I guess we'll be going," said Dee. She started around the van toward the driver's door.

The expression on Locke's face grew from a frown to a scowl. "You're not to leave town, remember?" he asked Harley.

"Don't worry," said Harley. "I won't go far."

"You'd better be sure of that," said Locke. He leaned in close to Harley. "We'll be watching you, Ms. Vincent."

The detective's badgering raised a spark of anger in Harley. "How nice," she said. "It's good to know that you haven't got anything better to do. This must be a really safe town."

The detective's lip curled in contempt. Then he spun around and walked away, the heels of his shoes clacking against the sidewalk.

Harley watched the man until he went out of sight around a corner, then she climbed into the passenger seat. From across the van, Dee was looking at her with a strange expression.

"What is it?" asked Harley.

"Arson and murder?" Dee said.

Harley shrugged. "They think I might have started the fire at the bookstore."

"Yeah?" Dee cranked the engine of the van. "Well,

it's nice to see that you've been making new friends."

They rolled out onto a crowded interstate as Scott gave directions from the back of the van. Gradually, the spark of light shifted toward the center of the screen. As it did, it gradually grew brighter.

"The point seems to be pretty steady," Scott said as he leaned over the display. "The best I can measure, it's about point-four-two H-units."

"Point-four-two what?" asked Harley.

"H-units." Scott looked up from his display. "Your output seems pretty steady, so I used you to calibrate the system. I'm measuring other people's output in Harleys."

Harley squeezed her eyes shut. "Oh, great. Now I'm a measuring stick."

"It looks like we've got about a mile to go," said Scott.

"What a coincidence," said Dee. She pointed at a sign beside the road. "It's exactly a mile to the airport."

The closer they got to the airport, the brighter the point became. "Do you think Billie might be trying to leave town?" Scott asked.

"I'm not sure," said Harley. She glanced at the side-view mirror and examined the road behind her for a familiar sedan. "Let's just hope that Detective Locke doesn't think I'm trying to make a break for it."

The brightening point led them down the ramp and toward the short-term parking garage. Harley found herself getting increasingly nervous as they grew closer—and increasingly angry. Billie had kidnapped Noah and had tried to kill Harley. And she had lied to them both, trying to gain Harley's sympathy and worm her way into Noah's affections.

"Be careful," she said as they slipped into the shadows under the concrete roof of the garage. "Billie is capable of anything."

"I didn't like her from the beginning," said Dee. "I knew she was trouble." She drove the van slowly between rows of parked cars.

"We're close," said Scott in a soft voice.

Harley strained to see through the van window but could make out nothing but dark, empty cars. "Where?"

"Ten meters," said Scott. "Now eight."

Dee slowed the van to a crawl. "I don't see anything."

"Five meters," Scott called. "Four."

Harley turned quickly from side to side, and even looked up at the ceiling. The garage appeared to be empty. "Where is she?"

"Three meters," said Scott. He raised his gaze up from the screen and shook his head. "We're right on top of it."

Dee stopped the van. "If there's someone here we must be sitting on them."

Harley stared through the side window and twisted around in her seat. "I don't . . . ," she began. Then something caught her eye. She pointed to the right. "Over there," she whispered.

Dee leaned toward her from across the van. "What? I don't see anything."

"The driver's door on that car is open," Harley replied. She pointed at a silver Mazda coupe. "Just a crack."

"Really?" Dee looked for a moment longer, then nodded. "Good spotting."

Harley turned away from the door. "All right," she said. "What do we have for weapons?"

Dee exchanged a glance with Scott. "Weapons?"

"Does that mean you didn't bring any weapons?" Harley asked. "Kenyon had enough guns in the house to outfit an army, and you didn't bring any of them?"

"We came out here to find you," said Dee. "We weren't expecting a gun fight."

"Great." Harley glanced at the silver car. Billie had proved inhumanely tough, and her comrades at Umbra had carried weapons powerful enough to turn a person into ash. "Have we got *anything* we could use?"

Scott scrambled to the back of the van. "There's a big medical kit back here," he called. "There are a couple of syringes filled with some pretty heavy sedatives."

The idea of facing Billie with nothing but a needle didn't seem like the most appealing thing Harley had ever considered. She wondered for a moment if they should leave. They could go and find better weapons, then come back. Then she looked back at the car with the open door.

Billie was here. If Harley left, Billie might get out of the car, go into the airport, and catch a flight to the other side of the world. Harley might never get a chance to make Billie pay for what she had done.

"Give me the syringe."

Scott climbed up to the front of the van and handed over the sedative. "Be careful with this," he warned. "The dose in here is about five times normal. If you jab yourself, you'll get really sleepy really fast."

"Got it," said Harley. She took a careful grip on the syringe and started to open the door.

"Wait," said Dee. "Don't you want us to go with you?"

Harley shook her head. "Stay here. I want you out of here if something goes wrong."

"If something goes wrong," said Dee, "we'll make sure she pays."

"Thanks," said Harley. She pushed open the door and stepped out of the van. "Let's just hope nothing goes wrong."

She advanced toward the silver car with her pulse thrumming in her throat. At first, the car appeared empty. Then Harley spotted a shadowy form slumped down in the front seat. She raised the syringe and held it out in front of her. It was hard to figure out what Billie was doing. It had to be some kind of trap.

"You might as well come out," said Harley. She tried to make her voice firm and hoped that Billie couldn't hear the tremble beneath the surface. "I see you in there."

For a moment, there was no reaction. Then the car door swung slowly open.

Harley raised the syringe, ready to strike.

"Harley?" a rasping voice asked. A spider-thin hand emerged from the car, then a long leg that was far too skinny for the pants leg around it.

Harley slowly lowered her arm. "Cain?" she whispered.

Agent Ian Cain slowly unfolded from the car. Cain was as tall as ever, but if anything, he looked even worse than he had the last time Harley had seen him in Stone Harbor. The agent's face was sunken and hollow-cheeked. His eyes were dull, and his expression seemed stunned.

"Harley, is that you?" he croaked.

"It's me," Harley replied. The sight of Cain brought a flurry of emotions. The agent had helped her in the past—even saved her life. But he'd also led her into insanely dangerous situations without giving her all the information she needed to know. And if she hadn't been trying to find blood for him and investigate the schism within his organization, Kenyon would still be alive. "How did you get here?" she asked.

Cain's shoulders sagged and he leaned his weight against the car door. "I was looking for you." His voice was no more than a wheeze.

Harley turned and stepped back to the van. She

had mixed feelings about the agent, but she was not going to let him die on the floor of a garage. "It's Cain!" she shouted. "Come on, he needs help."

Together with Dee and Scott, Harley managed to help the staggering agent into the back of the van. Once inside, Cain lay with his eyes closed. His breath came in short, dry rattles.

"We've got to give him the fluid," Harley decided. "Does that medical kit of yours have what you need to do a transfusion?"

"I'm not sure," said Scott. "I think so."

"Then let's do it right now."

Cain suddenly opened his eyes and reached up a bony hand to grab Harley by the arm. "No," he said. "You've got to . . . move. They'll be . . . coming for me."

"What do we do?" asked Dee.

Harley bit her lip. "Let's close up and get on the road. We can try to get the transfusion going once we're out of here."

Dee nodded. "Do you know how to do it?"

"I have absolutely no idea," answered Harley.

"Then maybe you better drive," said Dee. "I've picked up a little from the EMTs who work with my father. I can help Scott get things started."

Harley hurried around to the front of the van and cranked the engine. When all the doors were closed and Cain was resting as comfortably as possible on the narrow corridor in the center of the van, she pulled out and left the airport.

"How's it going back there?" she called.

"We're just getting started," said Dee. "You have any idea how to open this little pop bottle you stole?"

The flask of artificial blood had survived an explosion and a lot of rough handling without breaking. "Nope," Harley replied.

"We'll figure out something."

A few minutes later, both Dee and Scott gave a little shout of triumph as they managed to crack open the vial. Shortly after that they got the transfusion underway.

"It's going in fast," Dee reported from the back of the van. "I sure hope this is the right stuff."

"Me too," Harley whispered under her breath. She wondered if she was doing the right thing helping Cain. Kenyon had argued that they should let Cain die. Harley had won that argument, but now Kenyon was gone. Harley felt a jab of regret. If she hadn't listened to Cain, they would all still be in Stone Harbor, and Kenyon would still be alive.

She drove the van back onto the interstate and turned toward the core of the city. Traffic was light, and she drove slowly to keep the ride as smooth as possible.

"The fluid is almost all in him," Dee called. "Cain's still zonked, but I think he's looking better."

Suddenly Harley heard a shuffling and thumping from the back of the van. She twisted her neck to look behind her. "What's going on?"

In the narrow space, Scott scrambled to get past

Cain. "Something's wrong," he muttered. "Really wrong."

Harley glanced at the road for a moment. Everything was clear for hundreds of yards in front of her except for a single black Corvette prowling along the lane to her left. She looked back at Scott. "What is it?"

"Take a look," he said. Scott lifted the screen of his handmade paranormal detector and turned it around so Harley could see. The entire screen was one huge smear of white.

"What does that mean?" asked Harley, glancing momentarily back at the road.

Scott shook his head. "I don't know."

"Is it broken?"

"I don't think so. I think—" Scott stopped and looked at Harley with fear in his blue eyes. "I think there's something out there."

Harley turned back to the highway and stretched her neck as she looked from side to side. "I don't see anything."

"It's there," Scott insisted.

The black Corvette switched to the lane in front of the van. Harley squinted through the small back window of the sports car. She could just make out the silhouette of two figures. The one on the passenger side was moving. He was doing something. He was—

Watch out, screamed a voice in Harley's mind.

She jerked the wheel left just as a hand emerged

from the right side of the Corvette. For a moment, the space between the van and the sports car seemed to ripple like the air over a hot stove. Then the van's windshield imploded into a thousand tiny fragments of glass.

The steel beam at the right of the windshield crumpled as if kicked by an invisible mule. The empty passenger seat ripped free of its mounts and flew backward in a flurry of shredded vinyl and foam.

Harley grabbed the wheel as the van skidded left, then right, and then rocked up on its wheels and nearly rolled over. Screams filled the air. Harley realized one of them was hers.

The van's right wheels left the pavement. The heavy vehicle clipped the end of a metal barrier and charged down a hill, throwing up a stream of mud. Harley fought to hang on as they bumped over grass.

With the wind whipping in her face through the shattered windshield, Harley stomped the gas and zoomed down the hill as fast as the damaged van could handle.

Selena stomped the brakes, and the car skidded to a stop along the shoulder of the road. "Hurry!" she cried. "They're getting away."

Kenyon shoved another of the dart-shaped rounds into the strange gun and leaned through the open window of the Corvette. He pressed two fingers against the buttons on the weapon as he prepared to fire.

The van was careening wildly down a grassy slope. The vehicle's tires threw up geysers of grass and mud as it bounced toward a line of shrubs.

"Fire!" shouted Selena. "They're almost out of range."

Kenyon nodded, but as he sighted down the length of the tiny gun, the little weapon seemed to gain a thousand pounds of weight. Sweat rolled into his eyes and butterflies did a full-fledged ballet in his stomach.

Ever since his parent's death, Kenyon had practiced with different weapons for the time when he would get a chance at revenge. He had blasted away a thousand targets and had even exchanged shots with the soldiers of Unit 17. Shooting at the van had been different.

According to Selena, the ammo fired by the gun

contained a highly concentrated packet of magnetic monopoles. When fired, the invisibly small particles expanded rapidly, distorting not just the objects they struck, but the very space they passed through. Kenyon was sure that Scott would have been thrilled by all the technical details, but to him they meant very little. All he really understood was the result.

The blast of the gun had hit the front of the van like a rampaging elephant. The driver had swerved left at the last minute, dodging a direct hit. Even so, the effects had been impressive. The windshield had been nearly vaporized, the front grill smashed, the right corner of the van crumpled. Kenyon had glimpsed only the shadowy shape of the driver through the shattered windshield before the van had swerved, skidded, and veered from the pavement.

"Shoot!" cried Selena. "Are you a coward? Shoot!"

Kenyon fired.

The tiny, tube-shaped gun jumped in his hands as the rippling wave of twisted space and matter flew through the air toward the fleeing van. But Kenyon's shot struck the ground well behind the van, raising a fountain of dirt and grass.

When the air cleared, Kenyon saw that the van had reached an access road that ran beside the highway. With a squeal of tires the vehicle roared out of sight.

"What was *that?*" Selena asked, her voice dripping with disgust. "Just what did you think you were doing?"

Kenyon shook his head. "I missed," he said. "That's all."

Selena made a noise that was just short of a growl. "You missed, all right," she spat. "You didn't even *try* to hit them." She climbed out of the car, walked around to Kenyon's side, and jerked open the door. "Give me that weapon!" she demanded.

Kenyon handed over the small gun. Selena snatched it from his hand and picked up the box of ammunition. "Don't you understand who was inside that van?"

"Cain," said Kenyon.

Selena nodded. "That's right. And not only Cain. There were others in there. From the information we were able to gather, the people in that van were some of the leaders of Cain's organization. They were the same ones that ordered the death of your friend Harley."

"I don't know." Kenyon looked at the path that the van had torn in the grassy hillside.

"You don't know?" Selena snapped. "You don't know *what?*"

Kenyon shook his head. "Shooting at soldiers doesn't bother me. But this wasn't fighting, this was an ambush."

Selena slammed her hand against the hood of the car. "Of *course* it was an ambush!" she shouted. "Do you realize how powerful Cain's organization is, or the kind of weapons they can use against us?"

"I know, but—"

Selena sighed and knelt down beside Kenyon. "Look, if you're searching for some wonderful little chess game where everyone plays by the rules, you're not going to find it."

Kenyon swallowed and looked down at the side of the highway. "I know," he said. "It just seemed . . . wrong."

"It *is* wrong," Selena agreed. "This is a secret war, but it's still a war. It's a dirty little war. And if we want to win this war, we're going to have to fight just as nastily as Unit 17, or Legion, or Cain. Do you understand?"

He nodded. "I understand."

"Good." Selena reached out and put her smooth, firm hands on either side of his face. "Can I count on you?"

Kenyon gazed up at her. In the daylight, Selena's dark eyes had another color at their core, a blue-green shade he had never seen before. A shadow of angry red desire coursed through him, driving away the shaky nerves and the guilt he had been feeling. "Yeah. Yeah, you can count on me."

"That's what I want to hear." Selena rocked forward on her feet and landed a hard kiss on Kenyon's mouth.

At the touch of her lips, the strange mixture of rage and desire flared again. Kenyon felt every muscle in his body tighten, and there was a buzzing in his ears. Cars whipped by on the highway behind him, but he paid them no attention. He reached out to Selena and tried to pull her close.

She slipped from his grip, and stepped back, laughing. "You seem to have recovered from your doubts."

"Yes," Kenyon said firmly. He could feel liquid fire moving through his veins. It burned away his guilt, his regrets, all the weakness that had held him back. All that was left was boiling fury and his desire for Selena.

"The next time you get a chance to kill Cain," Selena asked, "will you take it?"

"Yes," Kenyon said promptly. He grinned a hard, hungry grin. "I won't miss again. Next time I'll crush Cain."

"Perfect," purred Selena. "And Unit 17?"

"Kill them," Kenyon replied eagerly.

"And Legion?"

"Kill them!"

"And Tessera, and all the others who try to stop us?"

Kenyon felt a blazing, mindless, violent joy. "Kill them all!" he cried.

Selena threw herself into his arms, pushing Kenyon back against the padded car seat. "Wonderful," she said as she kissed Kenyon's lips, and face, and neck. "You'll have revenge for your Harley."

For a moment, the name threw a bucket of water onto the blaze of his rage, but as Kenyon pressed his face into Selena's hair, that water vanished like it had fallen into the sun. Selena smelled like life and energy—like power. "Who is Harley?" he asked, his lips against the skin of Selena's neck.

"No one," Selena replied. "Never mind."

Kenyon pressed his fingers into her back, digging

into the muscles there as he pulled her close. She turned her face up to him, and again their lips met in a hard, lingering kiss.

The snug space inside the Corvette seemed to pulse and shift. For a moment, the woman in Kenyon's arms seemed . . . different. Smaller. Paler. Her eyes burned with a blue-green fire. In those eyes, Kenyon seemed to see a march of endless centuries and deathless cruelty.

He clamped his eyes shut and shoved her away, breathing hard.

"What's wrong?" asked Selena.

He shook his head. "I don't know."

"Kenyon, look at me. Come on, look at me."

Kenyon opened his eyes. Selena stood in front of him—tall and lovely, strong and soft. Her eyes were dark, her skin a deep and even tan.

"Are you all right?" she asked.

"Yeah." Kenyon rubbed at his eyes. He felt dizzy and confused. He tried to remember what he had been thinking only moments before, but it was hard to remember. It was hard to remember anything. "I guess I'm just tired," he said with a sigh.

"Then we should see that you get some rest," said Selena. She walked back around the car and climbed behind the wheel. "We need to prepare for tonight."

"What's happening tonight?" asked Kenyon.

Selena looked at him and smiled. "If I'm right," she replied, "tonight you'll get a second chance at Cain."

"Hold still," Dee ordered.

Harley gritted her teeth and concentrated on the trees outside the van's smashed window as tweezers dug into her arm and pulled out another jagged fragment of glass. They had been sitting in the van beside a lake in a county park for several minutes, and Dee still wasn't through with the first aid. "Why does it seem like we've done this before?"

Dee extracted the glass fragment and dropped it into a empty soda can with a clank. "Because you're good at getting hurt, and I'm good at doctoring you up." She leaned in close and peered at Harley's forearm. "All right. I think we're done. Let me go get the bandages, and we'll get you cleaned up and closed up." Dee put down her instruments, slid out the passenger door, and started around the side of the van.

In the corridor through the center of the van, an operation of a different sort was underway. Flying glass and a shredded chair had rendered Scott's detection device deader than a doornail. He sweated over its remains with soldering iron and spare parts.

In the second chair sat Ian Cain. The infusion of the green fluid had worked wonders for the agent, and his recovery was still continuing. With every passing moment Cain's flesh was more solid, his muscles more filled out, and his face more animated. As Harley watched, the fine lines around the agent's eyes grew smooth, and the color of his skin went from ash gray to a healthy tan. There was a new spark of energy in his eyes. Cain didn't look quite so young or quite so healthy as he had on the day when Harley first met him, but he looked a thousand percent better than he had a few minutes before. Considering the state he had been in when they found him at the airport, his recovery was a major miracle.

On one level, Harley was glad to see the agent alive. There was no doubt that Cain would be helpful if they had to face Billie. But on a deeper level, the sight of the agent breathing brought Harley a deep and pounding feeling of injustice. The members of the secret groups all seemed to have abilities that put them well outside the range of normal humans. It seemed completely wrong that Kenyon should be dead and Cain still alive.

"You know," said Cain, "your friend here is quite a genius." He nodded toward Scott. "Absolutely brilliant."

Dee looked in through the back of the van and grinned. "I always thought so," she said as she grabbed the medical kit. Dee and Scott had been together almost from the moment they set eyes on each other, and there wasn't much Dee liked better than bragging about Scott.

"Yes, and now it's obvious to me as well," Cain

continued. "For decades, we've known that some people had the gift for sensing others with paranormal ability, but I don't think anyone's ever developed a technological device with the same ability. If this creation of his works, it'll be a major advance."

"It works," said Scott. He held a magnifying lens up to his eye and brought the tip of the soldering iron into contact with some component so small that Harley couldn't even see it. "And as soon as I get this back together, you'll see that for yourself."

Dee stepped back through the passenger door and crouched in the spot where the chair had been. The blast that had taken out the windshield had sent the seat flying all the way to the back of the van. Fortunately, no one had been hurt by the flying upholstery, but the seat had been much too mangled to return to its former spot. Now there was only a set of four twisted bolts on the floor of the van to mark the place where the passenger chair had been.

"This will only take a second," said Dee. She ripped open a metallic packet, unfolded a sheet of sterile cotton soaked in alcohol, and began to wash the blood from Harley's arms.

Harley jerked back. "That stings."

"Oh, don't be a baby," Dee chided. She dabbed at the edge of the cuts, then reached into the kit for a tube of antibiotic. "You should be glad they use safety glass in cars. If that had been regular plate glass, it would have cut you to ribbons."

"Thanks," said Harley. "I knew I could count on you for a comforting thought."

"There!" Scott called triumphantly. "That should do it." He put down his soldering iron and flipped a switch at the side of the device.

Harley twisted her head around and saw the screen flash white for an instant, then go completely dark. "Where are all the spots we saw before?" she asked.

"I added a filter while I was at it," said Scott. "It allows me to regulate a minimum energy level for display. Ordinary people won't register at this level."

"What about me and Cain?"

"You're there." Scott pointed to a very faint point in the center of the screen. "I have to keep it turned way down, or the source we detected before will swamp everything else."

Cain got up from his chair. He crouched to fit under the low roof and shuffled over to stand beside Scott. "Just how powerful is this anomalous reading you encountered?"

Scott shrugged. "Hard to tell until we find it again." He began twisting the center knob. Almost instantly a brilliant blob of light appeared in the lower right corner. "There!" he exclaimed. "I'm getting a reading of over ninety H-units."

"H-units?" Cain inquired.

Harley groaned. "Please, don't ask."

Scott studied the screen for a moment longer, then pointed through the shattered windshield of the van. "It's over that way," he said. "Southeast of our position."

Harley looked at the spot on the display screen. It moved slowly toward the edge of the screen and disappeared. Scott grabbed the knob and twisted again until the light reappeared. "It seems to be in motion. Traveling west."

"How far away is this energy source?" asked Cain.

Scott traced his finger across the glass of the screen. "With all the adjustments I've made, it's hard to be sure, but I'd guess it's about twenty miles from us."

"What do we do now?" Dee asked. "Is that spot Billie?"

Cain shook his head slowly. "I don't know. The individual that you call Billie is . . . exceptional. But I have no way of comparing the readings Mr. Handleson is making to my knowledge of this individual."

Dee finished wrapping the bandages around Harley's forearms and taped them closed. Harley turned and sat looking backward with her knees in the chair and her aching arms folded across the headrest. Cain was staring intently at the point on the screen, watching as Scott made one adjustment after another to keep the light in view.

"We will have to approach the position cautiously," said Cain. "If this is the target we're after, she'll be expecting us. You must follow my directions very carefully."

The agent's confident tone brought Harley's anger back to the surface. "Who put you in charge?"

Cain glanced at her for only a moment before turning back to the screen. "Experience puts me in charge, Ms. Davisidaro."

"Experience," Harley repeated. "Our recent experience with you hasn't been so good."

"What do you mean?"

"In Stone Harbor. What happened? Where did you go?"

Cain turned around to face her. "The substitute material obtained by Mr. Handleson and Ms. Janes provided a brief burst of energy. I roused myself enough to administer the remainder, then made my departure."

Harley frowned. "You mean you sneaked out without telling anyone."

Cain's expression became cold. "I thought it best that I get out quickly without wasting time on conversation. I had possible information sources to check."

"I'm sure you did," Harley replied. "But that's no excuse. You came to me for help."

"I did—" Cain began.

Harley cut him off. She had been bottling up a well of anger since Kenyon's death, and now it came pouring out. "Ever since we met, you've been popping in and popping out whenever you wanted. You never stop to explain anything, and I'm not sure I can trust what you do say."

Cain frowned. "Ms. Davisidaro, I—"

"Kenyon and I traveled across the country to try to help you," Harley continued, cutting off the agent's words. "You wanted us to stop the conspiracy in your group. Well, we tried. And while we were trying, I was shot at, taken prisoner, and threatened with torture."

"I never intended—"

"Shut up!" Harley shouted. "Just shut up." She sat for a moment, breathing hard as she tried to regain enough composure to go on. "Kenyon . . . Kenyon gave his *life* helping you. He didn't even trust you, but he went anyway . . . and . . . and they killed him." She squeezed her eyes shut against the tears welling in her eyes. She didn't want to cry. Not now. "He gave his life, and you couldn't even be bothered to let us know what was going on."

For long seconds, there was silence in the van. Twice, Cain opened his mouth as if he was about to say something, then closed it again.

Finally, he cleared his throat and spoke. "You're right. I should have let all of you know what I was doing. I've worked on my own for a long time, Ms. Davisidaro. I'm not used to explaining my actions to anyone."

"That's no excuse," Harley snapped.

"I know."

Harley stared into the agent's face and felt a new anger rising. "Tell me something, why did you come to me?"

"I was injured," said Cain. "I couldn't trust the others in my own organization, so I thought—"

"Not then," Harley interjected. "I mean the very first time. Why did you come to me back on the Tulley Hill military base after my father disappeared?"

Cain spread his long hands across the workbench and looked down. "I came to you because your father was involved with Unit 17. I thought I might help you retrieve your father, and in return you might provide me with valuable information."

"Liar," said Harley.

Cain winced. "I assure you—"

"Don't assure me of anything." Harley pounded her fist against the side of the van. "You didn't just want information from me, and you didn't try to rescue my father. You *used* me. You used Noah and me to stop Unit 17. And you tried to use me and Kenyon to stop Tessera. That's the truth, isn't it?"

Cain nodded slowly. "Yes."

"Because you thought we were disposable."

"Yes."

"And I was an idiot," said Harley. "I let you use me. I almost *begged* for it. Even when you showed up today, I was still ready to believe you were our friend." She shook her head hard, and the hot tears flew away from her face. "You just want to use us again—to throw us out like bait to catch some monster."

This time Cain was silent. He walked slowly back

143

to the rear chair and sat down, but he did not answer Harley's accusation.

Harley stared at him and felt a acid mix of hurt and guilt eating at her guts. "I wanted someone to help me find my father, then someone to help me find Noah. I thought you were that someone. Now they're both gone. And because of me, Kenyon is dead."

Cain's head came up quickly. "No," he said. "Mr. Moor's death is not your responsibility. I was the one that sent you on that mission."

"It *is* my fault," Harley replied. "Kenyon didn't trust you. He went because I was going. He died because of me."

Cain started to respond, but Harley didn't want to hear any more. She spun around and hurled open the door of the van, then she jumped out and began to run.

She ran without looking back. At first, each breath she took came out as a sob. As long as she had kept the emotions inside, everything had seemed all right, but once she had opened the tap, they seemed to rush out like a tidal wave.

There was a paved path between the trees, but Harley ignored it. She ran across fields and splashed through a shallow stream. As her legs began to grow warm and loose, she lengthened her stride and pushed up a hill. The marble bulk of a museum went by on her right. Harley kept running. She dashed across a fairway in front of a foursome of startled golfers and passed the bowl of a great open-air ampitheater. Finally, she reached the edge of the park.

For a moment, Harley thought of just running on. She would run for days, and leave Harley Davisidaro far behind. She would change her name again and start over in a new town. With a fresh start. A new life.

But in the end she turned and began to run back the way she came.

By the time she came in sight of the van, Harley's legs had began to tire and her anger was exhausted. Agent Cain stood outside the vehicle, waiting as Harley approached.

"Are you all right, Ms. Davisidaro?" he asked.

Harley nodded. "Yes."

Cain's lips flattened into a thin line. "You were right about what you said before. I've been trying to make you into my tool to use against Umbra and the others. The death of your friend is on my head."

"No," said Harley. "I was wrong."

"Everything you said was true."

"It was true, but I didn't say everything." Harley walked closer to the agent and stood looking up into his sharp-chinned face. "I've known from the beginning that you were trying to use me, and I was trying to use you. We both had our own goals, and we used each other to try and reach those goals. Isn't that the way the game is played?"

The agent nodded. "I suppose it is." He turned away and took a few steps toward the trees. "It's a messy game, Ms. Davisidaro. A very ugly game. I believe I'm about ready to retire."

"Retire later," said Harley. "First you've got to help us stop Billie."

"No," said Cain.

Harley frowned. "What do you mean, *no?* I thought you had a plan."

"I had a *scheme,*" said the agent, "not a plan. "Just as you said, I had an intention to dangle you in front of Billie and see how she reacted." He shook his head. "I've decided not to carry out that scheme. The best thing for you to do now is go home."

Harley tightened her hands into fists. "We're going down there to face Billie."

"Then you're going without my orders and without my aid," said Cain. "I'll not see you get killed for this." The agent stepped into a small grove of trees and disappeared among the trunks.

Harley hurried after him. "We have to go," she said. "We have to stop Billie before she takes over your organization and learns all the secrets you've collected."

She stepped around the tree where she had seen the agent vanish, but there was no sign of the tall man. The little patch of forest was green and silent.

"Cain!" Harley shouted. She received no answer but the whistle of the wind.

After a few minutes, she gave up and returned to the van. Harley looked in through the side door. Dee and Scott were sitting close together in the back. There was a spread of computer components on the workbench, but Harley was willing to bet that they had been discussing something other than electronics.

"Where's Cain?" asked Scott. "Did you talk to him?"

Harley nodded. "We talked. He's gone."

Dee's eyebrows rose up her forehead. "You didn't kill him, did you?"

Harley couldn't help but laugh. "No, I didn't kill him."

"That's good." Dee gave a dramatic shiver. "Remind me never to get on your bad side."

"What are we going to do now?" asked Scott.

Harley thought for a moment. "Cain seemed pretty convinced that if we go up against Billie, we'll get ourselves killed."

"And?" asked Dee.

"And, I don't care what Cain thinks." Harley looked at the display on the screen. The white dot was gone. "What happened to your machine? Did you lose the signal?"

"Sort of," said Scott. "It reached a point downtown, held position for a few minutes, then disappeared. I haven't seen any sign of it since."

Harley looked at the blank screen. "Maybe she has some kind of hideout, like the underground place where Mr. Antolin lived. That might block your signal."

"It's possible," Scott agreed. "Like I said, I don't understand this energy very well."

"In any case, it looks like our best bet is to go to the point where you got your last reading." Harley pushed her hair back from her face and took a deep breath. "I'm going down there."

"And if it's Billie?" asked Dee.

"If it's Billie," Harley said, her hands tightening into fists, "then I'm going to take her out any way I can. I don't expect either of you to come with me."

"I'm going," Dee said quickly.

Scott nodded. "Me too. Kenyon was my friend. If this Billie had something to do with him getting killed, I should be there."

Harley thought about trying to talk them out of it, but she stopped herself. She was not going to be like Cain. She wouldn't trick them into going, and she wouldn't make them stay. It was their own decision.

Driving the van without a windshield presented something of a challenge. At any speed above twenty miles an hour, the wind roared through the vehicle. Harley's hair whipped around her face as she drove along the streets heading toward the heart of the city. It was like driving her motorcycle, only worse. She had no helmet to protect her face from the buffeting wind. The sides of the van sent the wind back to hit her from all directions. By the time they got within a block of their destination, she felt as if her skin had been scraped with steel wool.

It was after seven when they arrived downtown, and the offices and stores of the city were well on their way to being empty. Traffic in the streets was light. Harley pulled the van into an empty parking space and killed the engine.

"Which way?" she asked.

Scott pointed toward a tall building that seemed to be made of pink stone and gold-tinted glass. "As best I can tell, the source was over there."

Harley leaned her head back to look up at the top of the building. It reached above all the others and extended into a series of swooping peaks made from glass and steel. Despite the modern design, there was something terribly medieval about the building. Its stone sides reared above the city with the bulk of some ancient castle.

"I think this is the place," said Harley.

Dee crunched through the broken glass as she came to the front of the van. "I don't suppose we discovered any weapons along the way."

Harley shook her head. "No. Not really."

"We go in together," Scott called from the back of the van. "Like the Three Musketeers."

"That's cool," said Dee, "but the Musketeers had guns and swords."

Scott came forward to crowd into the front with Dee and Harley. "Maybe we should consider this a reconnaissance mission," he suggested. "We go in, we take a look, and we figure out what kind of tools we need to handle a confrontation on our next visit."

"All right," said Harley. But in her heart, she felt a pressure building, a tingling in the air like the feeling before a summer thunderstorm. She doubted there would be another visit. "Let's go."

They piled out of the van and walked toward the building Scott had pointed out. With every step, Harley became more certain that they were going to the right place. She could feel that invisible pressure gathering within her with every step she took. There was something here, something that was aware of them—something that was waiting for them.

The revolving door turned, pushing them into a huge vaulted lobby lined with smooth, polished gray and white stone. A security guard at the other side of the huge room gave the trio a curious look but made no immediate move to evict them.

Harley walked slowly across the empty lobby. The floor under her feet was cut in a design that was hard to see. There was a subtle interplay of colors, light gray, then white, then cream. She looked down at the edges of the design as they passed under her feet and tried to imagine what she would see if she could be suspended from the high ceiling of the room. She couldn't be certain, but she had the feeling that the complete design would form something monstrous, something as huge and frightening as the beast she had seen in Umbra's underground headquarters.

"Where to now?" asked Dee.

Harley looked at the bank of brass elevator doors that lined the walls of the lobby. The unnamed sense in her mind that told her something powerful was in the building left no doubt about which direction they should go. "Up," she said. "All the way to the top."

The elevators were arranged by floor. The first ones they passed went only to the lower floors. Each successive elevator went to higher floors. At the far end of the lobby was a single elevator set away from all the others. In front of the elevator waited a figure in a trench coat and fedora.

Dee planted her hands on her hips. "Look who's here."

Agent Cain nodded to them in greeting. "So you decided to go through with it."

Harley stopped in front of the agent and scowled up at him. "Do you ever stop testing people?"

"If this was a test of common sense," replied Cain, "then you've all failed." He gestured toward the elevator. "She's waiting up there for you. Surely you know this is a trap?"

"I know," said Harley.

"And you're going anyway."

Harley pointed toward the ceiling. "She's up there. I'm not going to let her get away."

Cain showed a very rare smile. "I don't believe that letting this person *escape* should be among your concerns." He reached into the inner pocket of his jacket and produced a trio of small silver tubes. "However, if you insist on going up there, you might find these of use."

Harley took one of the tubes from his hand. It looked much like an expensive ink pen, but she knew from experience that the little device was a weapon that could produce impressive bolts of lightning.

Dee stepped forward and took one of the weapons. "Cool," she said. "Harley told me about these."

"Remember," Cain said as he handed Scott the remaining weapon, "these are not toys. There is no safety. Take care that you don't use them on yourselves."

"And whatever you do, don't cross the streams," said Dee.

Cain's brow creased in puzzlement. "What?"

Dee rolled her eyes. "Don't you ever watch movies?"

"Rarely," said Cain. He reached up and touched the brim of his hat. "Good luck to you all. I hope to see you again." He pulled his trench coat closed and began to walk away.

Harley stared after him. "You're still not coming?"

"No," Cain said over his shoulder. "The rules of my organization do not permit this kind of direct interference in events. Even providing you with equipment is a major violation. Should I take more action at this point, there might be serious repercussions."

"But you came to us for help," said Harley. "Besides, your organization is destroyed. You said yourself that the damage that Billie has done will take years to repair."

"Yes," Cain agreed. "But I've lived by the rules of that organization for a long time. I don't think I can change now." He walked across the lobby, his heels ringing on the stone floor, and he stepped out through the revolving door.

Harley felt another burst of anger. In her experience, whenever someone started talking about following the rules, it was a sure bet that they were trying to get out of something dangerous. "Come on," she said. "Let's get up there."

The elevator opened at their approach, and closed again as soon as they were inside. With a knee-bending burst of speed, they rose toward the top of the building.

Harley held the lightning pen firmly. The feeling that of tension grew with every floor they rose past. "Be ready," she warned. "Billie might be waiting as soon as the doors open."

Dee and Scott stepped to the right side of the elevator, while Harley moved to the left. All of them stood tense and ready as the elevator slowed to a stop. With a soft hiss, the doors slid open.

Harley stared in surprise.

Golden sunlight filled the space in front of them. It spread across emerald green trees, tall ferns, clumps of shrubbery, and fields overgrown with prairie grass and wildflowers. A pair of heavy-bodied birds rose up from the grass near the elevator door. Their wings thumped against the air as they climbed into a sky topped by arching windows of tinted glass.

"Cool," said Dee. "It's like jungleland goes high-rise."

Harley took a step onto the stone path outside the elevator. The air in the place was warm and humid. "It's something," she said.

"Stop!" shouted a commanding voice.

A figure appeared at the edge of the forest. It was silhouetted by the light of the setting sun—a dark shape surrounded by a golden halo.

Despite the warm temperature inside the artificial jungle, a tremor of cold swept through Harley. She raised her left hand and shaded her eyes against the light. "Kenyon?" she breathed.

The gold-rimmed figure stepped forward, and Kenyon Moor was revealed. He was dressed in new black jeans and a matching T-shirt that clung tightly to his muscular chest and arms. The sunlight glinted red against his dark hair and left a spark of fire in his eyes.

Harley's heart jumped in her chest, and she felt a wave of dizziness so strong she nearly fell to the ground. For a moment, she thought it might be some kind of trick. Billie could change her appearance; maybe someone else from her organization was pretending to be Kenyon. But that moment of doubt passed, replaced by a joy so strong it was almost painful. Harley wanted to run to Kenyon, or to say something—anything—to tell him how relieved she was. But the strength of her emotion left her paralyzed. She could only stand and stare as Kenyon walked closer.

"It's Kenyon!" Dee cried joyfully.

Scott stepped out of the elevator. "Oh, man. I can't believe it. We thought you were dead!" For the first time since Harley had seen him in St. Louis, Scott's face was split by its usual wide grin. He took a step toward his friend.

Kenyon's arm rose, revealing a strange device in his hand. It looked something like a miniature clarinet, shiny black with a round opening at the end. "Stop," he said again.

Scott's long face slumped and his smile disappeared. "Kenyon, what's wrong?"

A cloud covered the sun, and Kenyon's shape went from bright to dark against the windows. "Drop your weapons," he said in a cold voice. "Drop them now, or I'll kill you all."

THIRTEEN

A war raged in the mind of Kenyon Moor.

Whirlwinds of confusion rose up, only to be smashed against towering cliffs of rage. The people in front of him were familiar, but he couldn't put a name to them. They were The Enemy. They were responsible for everything that had gone wrong in his life. They were the heart of his anger and the cause of his trouble.

His finger tightened on the button of the distortion gun. "Drop the weapons," he repeated. "Or die."

The enemy in the middle—the female enemy with dark hair—dropped her small silver gun to the ground. "Kenyon. It's us. What's wrong with you?"

Her voice brought a fresh wave of confusion and dizziness. She knew his name, but Kenyon didn't know hers. He turned away from her and directed his gun toward the tall, male enemy. "Your weapon. On the ground, now."

The tall enemy hesitated for a moment, then let his weapon fall. "It's me, Scott. Have you lost your memory?"

Scott. The name echoed through Kenyon's mind, stirring connections and still more confusion.

The shortest of the three enemies tried to slip

away behind a knot of bushes. The comforting wall of anger closed in, burning away Kenyon's doubts. He shifted to the left and raised his gun. "Hold it!" he shouted. "Hands up."

The small female enemy hesitated. She still held her weapon, and she started to turn.

Yes, thought Kenyon. Give me an excuse.

But at the last moment, the enemy dropped her weapon on the ground. "If this is a joke," she said, "it is definitely *not* cool."

Kenyon gestured with his weapon. "Line up," he said. "We're going for a walk."

"What's wrong with him?" the male enemy said to the dark-haired female.

"Be quiet!" Kenyon commanded. "No talking. Line up." The three enemies exchanged glances, but they lined up on the curving stone path. "Good. Now, we're going to—"

Before he could finish he sentence, the elevator door chimed again. Kenyon spun around as the doors opened and saw a tall African American man in a dark coat and hat. In one hand, the man held a wallet that was open to show a gold badge. In his other he held a heavy revolver.

"Police department!" the man shouted. "Everyone on the ground! Now!"

The anger in Kenyon's mind came to a quick boil. He turned to the policeman and raised his weapon.

"No! Kenyon, don't! I know him! That's Detective Locke!" The tall, dark-haired girl threw herself at

Kenyon and shoved his arm away just as he pressed the buttons on his weapon.

The blast of the distortion gun missed its intended target. Instead the swarm of subatomic particles boiled into the wall left of the door, ripping through the frame of the elevator and gouging a ten-foot gap in the rich cherry paneling. The backblast from the impact was still strong enough to knock both the policeman and the two other enemies from their feet. The air was filled with splinters of wood and twisted bits of brass.

The impact of the female enemy sent Kenyon reeling. He fell to the ground, his limbs tangled together with those of the girl as she pounded at the weapon in his hands.

Kill her, commanded a voice in Kenyon's mind.

His rage rose to a fever pitch. He let the empty weapon fall away, then turned his fury on the girl. He shoved his enemy aside, stiffened his fingers into a blade, and drove a blow into her stomach. The girl's mouth flew open and her eyes bulged. Gasping for air, she fell flat on her back in the high grass at the side of the trail.

Kenyon let out a cry that was half laughter, half a roar of triumph. He leaped onto the fallen girl and pinned her arms down under his knees. She was strong. Her legs pressed hard at the ground and she writhed under his weight, but Kenyon was relentless. He dug the fingers of his left hand deep into her black hair and forced her head back. Then he made a blade of his right hand and raised it above her head.

A smile stretched his face. "Now!" he crowed. "Now you die!"

The girl drew in a gasping breath. "Kenyon, don't. It's me. It's Harley."

Kenyon hesitated. Harley. The name stirred a storm of associations. He remembered running from danger, and a gunfight in the darkness, and struggling for his life. He had not been alone in those times. "Harley?" he whispered.

The anger in his mind crumbled like a tower of glass. It fell from him in bitter waves, leaving behind a rising tide of guilt and a dawning horror at what he had been about to do.

Something cold and hard was pressed against the back of Kenyon's neck. "All right, partner," said a deep, firm voice. "Get off the young lady right now. And keep your hands where I can see them."

For a second, Kenyon felt a return of his anger, but it was only a shadow of the rage that had driven him moments before. He looked down at Harley's face with a mixture of shame and painful joy. "I . . . I thought you were dead," he said. Right on the heels of that joy, came a fresh wave of excruciating guilt. I almost killed her, he thought. I almost killed her with my own hands.

Relief swept across Harley's features, and Kenyon saw the hint of tears glittering in the corners of her dark eyes. "No," she said, her voice still hoarse from Kenyon's blow. "I'm okay. I thought you were dead."

"Get up," insisted the voice at Kenyon's back.

Trembling in relief, Kenyon raised his hands and stood. He turned his head and saw Scott and Dee standing near the place where his shot had torn open the wall. There was a thin stream of blood running down from a cut on Scott's forehead, but he was glad to see that there were no other obvious injuries.

"Are you guys okay?" he asked.

"I think so," Scott replied.

Dee picked up her glasses and perched them on her nose. "What about you? Are you coming down out of the ozone?"

Kenyon was often irritated by Dee's sense of humor, but he was glad to hear that she was still joking. "Yeah. I think so."

The policeman grabbed Kenyon by the wrist and pushed him over against the wall. "Hands up and hold still," he demanded. "I don't know what's going on here, but we're all taking a trip downtown to sort this out."

"No," said Selena's clear, confident voice. "I don't believe we are."

Her words were amplified so loud they were almost painful. They seemed to come from everywhere and nowhere. Kenyon turned his head and saw that the policeman had dropped his wallet and was holding his revolver in both hands as his brown eyes scanned the forest.

"Who is that?" Locke muttered under his breath.

"This has been amusing," boomed Selena's voice. "But I'm afraid it's time for our little play to end."

A cold breeze blew through the artificial jungle.

In the space below the peaked glass of the roof, streamers of mist gathered and twisted as they wove themselves into gray tumbling clouds. Despite the orange sunlight still slanting in through the long windows, a shadow fell over the green space.

With it, a darkness fell in Kenyon's mind. He felt cold fingers sifting through his thoughts. A series of emotions came and went as if someone were throwing a string of switches. "She's coming," he whispered.

The trees in the forest shivered and waves rippled across the grass. From the shadowed depths of the wood, a thin, lithesome figure strolled calmly along the cobbled path.

Selena's black hair hung free in a thick curtain that moved and swayed around her body. She wore a short, sheer gown of shimmering red that ended high on her long, tan legs and draped against the curve of her hips. With her olive skin and her flashing brown eyes, she was still so beautiful that Kenyon found it hard to look away.

"Good evening," she called. Her voice was at a more human volume, but it held a richness and texture that Kenyon had never heard before.

Detective Locke lowered his weapon and stepped forward. "Angela?"

Selena smiled at him and held out her arms. "It's been a long time, Derrick."

"Angela," the policeman repeated. There was a tight chord of pain in his voice. "But . . . how can it be you? You're dead. I held you while you died."

161

"Of course it's me," said Selena. She crooked a finger toward the detective. "Come here, Derrick. Let me show you how much I've missed you."

A stunned, blank expression crossed the face of the policeman. The revolver slipped from his fingers and bounced in the grass. He stumbled toward her like a sleepwalker.

Kenyon reached out and snagged the back of the man's suit coat. "Wait," he said. "She's not who you think she is. Her name is Selena."

"No," said Harley. "That's Billie."

Kenyon turned to Harley in confusion. "But she doesn't look anything like how you described Billie."

Harley nodded. "I know. But it doesn't matter what she looks like. That's her."

Locke jerked free of Kenyon's grip. "I don't care what you say. That's my Angela." He stepped forward, gaining speed at every step.

Kenyon started to go after the man, but before he could move, a sharp pain shot through his head. *Don't worry,* said a voice that went though his brain like an ice pick. *You'll get your turn.*

Locke reached Selena and stumbled to a stop. Kenyon could see tears sliding down the man's cheeks as he reached out to her. "I've missed you so much."

"Yes," Selena said sweetly. "And I've missed you." She wrapped her arms around the policeman as if she was going to hug him, but as she pulled him closer, the policeman's feet actually left the ground.

Though she was half the size of Locke, Selena raised him into the air as if he were a child. She held him over her head and looked up, a broad smile on her face.

"Angie!" he cried. "Angela, what are you doing?"

"Just having a little fun, dear Derrick. You watched your precious Angela die in your arms. It seems only right that those arms should kill you." She smiled at him a moment longer, then threw the policeman away across the fields like a baseball outfielder making a throw to home. Locke sailed awkwardly thirty feet over the grass and fell heavily amid a clump of bright yellow flowers. He lay there, crumpled and still as a heap of laundry.

Selena turned back to Kenyon and the others. "Well," she said. "That's one down. Three to go."

Harley stepped forward. "We're not going to let you get away this time, Billie."

Selena threw back her head and laughed. "You really are a lot of fun, Harley. I'm almost going to be sorry when you're dead. Almost."

Kenyon felt a moment of dizziness and the pressure on his mind eased. He stepped up to join Harley. "Is she really Billie?" he asked.

Harley nodded. "She can change the way she looks, but I'd know her anywhere."

Selena started walking down the path again, sauntering slowly and casually. "But aren't you flattered with this look?" she asked. "I gave your friend Kenyon just what he wanted."

"And what was that?" asked Harley warily.

Selena looked down at herself and ran her hands along the silky side of the red dress. "Harley Davisidaro's body and a mind as full of hate as his own." She looked up and smiled. "I do think I improved on the packaging, though."

Kenyon's stomach tightened. He felt disgust. Disgust with Selena, but more with than that, disgust with himself. "You used something on me," he said. "Some kind of hypnosis."

Selena looked at him and licked her red lips. "I didn't use anything that wasn't already in you. I gave you exactly what you wanted, and you loved it, didn't you?" She lowered her voice to a husky whisper. "Couldn't you love me still?"

Kenyon felt again that sensation of fingers working deep in his mind. Red anger and dark desire bloomed. He wanted to say no, but if he had, it would have been a lie. "Yes," he admitted. "And hate you at the same time."

Selena laughed. "Maybe I'll keep you alive a little longer. You can be amusing."

Harley stepped in front of Kenyon. "No," she said firmly. "It ends here, Billie. This is between you and me. You leave the rest of them out of it."

Selena's lips formed into a pout. "This isn't about just you."

Kenyon looked on in amazement as Selena's features began to flow like candle wax before a flame. Her skin grew paler, and her dark hair grew short and red. In a space of moments, she lost six inches of height and twenty pounds of weight. The dark eyes brightened, becoming circles of brilliant turquoise.

Where the tall, sultry Selena had stood a moment before, there was now a small girl with bright red hair, a turned-up nose, and a delicate air. Despite the change in her appearance, she still held a feeling of boundless energy.

Billie shook a finger at Harley like a parent chiding a small child. "Jealousy does not become you, Harley. Just because I stole away your boyfriend, Noah, and then took Kenyon from you, there's no reason you should take it personally." She spread her arms in a broad gesture.

From the shadows of the trees, two dark forms appeared. The hulking shape of the shadow man lurched across the fields, the grass dying around its feet as it came. It walked up beside Billie and stood at her left hand in a circle of frost.

Then the grass at her right hand began to ripple with movement. The sleek muscular form of a black jaguar emerged from the grass and sat down on Billie's left. It regarded Kenyon and the others with burning yellow eyes.

Billie reached down and stroked the fur of the big cat. "Just to prove how fair I am," she said warmly. "I've decided not to play any favorites. This time, I'm not going to take prisoners or carry anyone away. This time I'm simply going to kill you all."

FOURTEEN

Harley glanced down at the grass. The lightning gun Cain had given her was down there somewhere, but she could see no sign of it in.

"Pay attention, Harley," Billie called. "You wouldn't want to be daydreaming when it comes time to die."

The shadow man started up the path. Rocks snapped and cracked under its icy step, and a white trail of frost followed in its wake. After taking a dozen steps, it left the path and began to move to the left, then it turned and began angling toward the four waiting people. Dee and Scott shifted their positions as the creature approached Harley and Kenyon. Even from twenty yards away, Harley could feel a cold breeze stretching out from the midnight body of the creature.

"Kenyon," she whispered without taking her eyes from the approaching creature. "Do you still have that gun?"

"It's around here somewhere," he replied. "I dropped it when you hit me. I've got another bullet for it, but there's no more in the gun. It fires only a single shot without reloading."

Billie laughed. "I know that seems like a pity now, but you should really be thankful. If it had fired any faster, Kenyon would have probably killed you all when he was shooting at your van."

Harley looked away from the approaching shadow man and stared at Kenyon in shock. "You shot the van?"

His face tightened in pain and he looked down at the ground. "I didn't know it was you, Harley, I swear."

"He didn't care!" Billie shouted in a teasing tone. "He was so in love with his Selena that he couldn't even remember your name!"

Harley turned back to see that the shadow man was only ten yards away. Thin streamers of fog swirled around the creature's icy body. Red sparks glowed deep in the shadows of its featureless face.

"All right," Harley told Kenyon, Scott, and Dee. "Everybody listen. Don't let it touch you. It's strong, and it's cold, but it's also slow. Stay away from it and you'll be all right."

"Ah," said Billie, "but you might not have that choice." She snapped her fingers, and the jaguar jumped up from her side.

The animal slunk quickly, circling around to the right and coming up along the wall. The cat held its head low, but its yellow eyes never left the group of people. A deep rumble came from its powerful chest, and its jaws opened to reveal brilliant white fangs of startling size.

Harley took a step back and found herself bumping into Kenyon. She could see what the creatures were doing. Between the shadow man, Billie, and the jaguar, the four of them were caught in a trap. She backed up against the shattered wall and looked for a route of escape.

The shadow man came closer, its dark hands reaching out. The muscles of the jaguar's shoulders bunched and eased as the big cat stalked them like prey. At the middle of the triangle Billie stood on the path with a smile on her face and a gleam in her eyes.

"Good-bye, Harley," she said. "Your blood, and that of your friends, will nourish the roots of this forest. Every time I walk in their shade, I will think of you."

"It's always nice to meet an ecologically correct psychopath," said Dee Janes.

The shadow man gave a rumbling growl and lunged forward. Its fingers stretched out toward Harley.

A bolt of crackling lightning shout out from the bushes behind the jaguar. The wriggling electric fire cut so close to Harley that she could feel the hairs on her neck rise. It slipped past Kenyon and struck the shadow man squarely in the chest.

Billie let out a warbling scream of rage as white fire played over the dark body of the shadow man. The creature staggered back, spun around and batted at the fire uselessly with its hands. The electricity kept coming.

As Harley watched, the shadow man began to shrink. Its towering height dropped to that of an average person. Its broad trunk became more narrow. For a fraction of a second, Harley saw not a shadow man, but a normal man standing in front of her. A man whose face was twisted in agony. Then there was a final flash of light, and the creature was completely gone.

Harley's heart soared as a tall figure stepped from behind a screen of shrubbery. "Cain!"

Agent Ian Cain touched a finger to the brim of his hat and nodded. "One down," he said. "Only two to go."

Billie spun to face him. "You! Why aren't you cowering in a corner somewhere, taking your little notes and sending in your little reports? Isn't that what you're supposed to do?"

Cain gave her a flat, professional smile. "On occasion, a little direct action seems like the proper course—even if it does go against the rules."

Billie's back arched and her chest heaved as she drew in deep angry breaths. "You've picked a very bad time to make your stand," she said, "and you've picked the wrong person to oppose." The strange wind rose again and the trees of the little jungle swayed. Overhead the miniature clouds grew darker, and Harley saw a flicker of lightning that did not come from a gun.

"We'll have to see about that," said Cain. He leveled his weapon and fired.

The lightning snapped and hissed through the air toward Billie. It surrounded her small form in a blanket of light so bright that Harley could see only a bare shadow of the woman inside.

"Aim for the flattop!" shouted Dee.

Harley looked over at her and shook her head. "You watch too many movies."

Dee shrugged. "It seemed appropriate. I've seen *Ghostbusters* like twenty-five times. And tell me Billie doesn't look like Gozer."

Cain walked toward Billie. He kept his weapon firing as he came, directing an unending stream of scalding electricity at the small woman. The stones on the path cracked open from the heat, and the grass nearby began to steam. Still Billie stood, wrapped in fire and light. Harley could see Billie's arms raising and falling, and over the sound of the lightning gun, she thought she heard a whisper of some rhythmic chant.

The lightning gun began to falter. The bolt it produced grew dimmer and bluer. Cain stood so close to Billie that his own hand was almost lost in the glow that surrounded her. Harley could see the electric wind blowing back Cain's hair and the bright blue glow reflected in the agent's eyes. His skin reddened from the heat of the assault.

Cain's jaw was clenched in determination. "Ms. Davisidaro," he shouted. "I think you should consider getting out of here now."

Harley looked around. The shot that Kenyon fired had left the elevator doors dented and stuck in a half-closed position. If there was another exit, it wasn't marked. It didn't look like anyone was getting off the floor any time soon.

There was a high-pitched squeal, then a loud pop. The lightning gun sputtered, squirted a last stream of blue glow, then died. For a moment, the glow remained around Billie's body. Slowly, it faded away. When it was gone, Harley saw Billie standing there just as she had before Cain fired. She was not injured. Even her gown was unscorched by the bath of fire.

She looked at Cain and shook her head sadly. "Is that all you've got?" she said. "Let me show you power." Billie made sharp gesture with her left hand.

A beam of red fire leapt from her fingers and surrounded the agent. Cain bellowed in pain as the fire lifted him from the ground. He rose higher and higher, until he was lost in the clouds overhead. Then Billie brought her hand down.

Cain came tumbling from the clouds like a comet scorching across the sky. Sparks trailed behind him and flames ran along his flapping coat. He struck the glass wall of the enclosed space with a sound like the ringing of a huge bell. Cracks spread from the top to the bottom of the tall window. A piece of glass the size of a dinner plate snapped free and went tumbling out into the air.

Agent Cain fell to the ground in a smoking heap and lay still.

Harley spotted the silver barrel of a lighting gun in the grass to her left. She dove to the ground and came up with the pen in her right hand. She rose up and aimed the device at Billie.

A dark blur crashed into her from the right. The pen went flying from her hand and Harley was sent sprawling into the grass. Hot breath steamed against her neck. She turned her head and found herself looking into the mad yellow eyes of the jaguar.

The big cat opened its mouth and hissed like a whole basketful of snakes. It bared fangs that were long, sharp, and blinding white.

Then a bolt of lightning touched the cat's side.

The jaguar jumped straight up twenty feet and came down running. It scuttled past Billie, past where Cain lay, and kept on running until it was lost in the forest.

Dee Janes let out a shout of triumph. "Momma may be immune to the these things, but it looks like kitty isn't!"

Kenyon reached down to Harley and helped her to her feet. Harley gave him a quick smile. "Two down," she said.

Billie turned to them. Her eyes were no longer just bright, they were blazing. Pale blue light beamed from her face that was strong enough to color the space around her. "You have no idea how pitiful your efforts are," she said. "Do you know who I am? Do you know *what* I am?" She sneered. "You think I'm part of Umbra, but I'm far older than Umbra. You have no idea how far I have come, or how long I have been here. I was worshiped when your ancestors were still squatting in caves!"

Billie raised her hands and red fire gathered around them. "I've wasted enough time on you," she said. "Die!" She brought her hands down, throwing out a beam of fire twice as wide as the one that had consumed Agent Cain.

Harley threw herself to the ground. The red beam that Billie threw ripped through the air inches above her head. The heat of its passing seared her back and drew the air from her lungs. She saw Dee Janes fire one of the lightning guns toward Billie, but the bolt of lightning missed, setting fire instead to a tree at her back. Billie snarled and turned toward Dee.

Something glittered on the ground beside Harley's face. She stretched out her hand and found the cold weight of Detective Locke's revolver. Harley picked it up quickly, thumbed back the hammer, sighted down the blue steel barrel, and fired.

Billie might have been immune to the effect of Cain's lightning gun, but good old-fashioned lead definitely had an impact. She screamed as the bullet tore through her red dress and through her thin frame. She whirled toward Harley.

Harley fired again.

Red light flared from Billie's body as the bullet struck home. Once again her skin rippled and melted. Billie's face transformed into that of a thin woman with sharp, dusky features, then into something that wasn't even remotely human. Her hair disappeared as her skull became long and flattened. Her skin took on a gray-green tone and grew rough and pebbled. Her face transformed into a long snout that was studded with cruel, hooked teeth. Only the eyes remained unchanged, glaring like turquoise flashlights above the snarling mouth.

The reptilian creature rose from the ground and hovered in a column of light. "You will know pain," it said in a rippling, hissing voice. "You will breathe pain as if it were the air."

Harley rose to her knees, steadied the gun with both hands, and took careful aim. "You first." She fired again.

The force of the shot drove the Billie-thing spinning through the air. Black fluid spilled between the snarling teeth and dripped onto the grass where it steamed and sizzled like acid.

The monstrous thing that had been Billie hung in the air, its wide mouth open as if it meant to bite Harley in half. It spread it clawed arms wide and roared with rage and pain.

Harley held the pistol in both hand and aimed at the low, scaley skull. One shot, right between those glowing eyes, should end this thing once and for all. "Good-bye, Billie," she said. "And good riddance."

Harley aimed carefully and pulled the trigger. The revolver gave only a dry click. She quickly pulled the trigger again. *Click*. And again. *Click*.

The gun was empty.

The creature gave a dry inhuman laugh. "Now," it said. "It's my turn." It raised its clawed hands. Red lightning ripped across the sky. Streamers of fire spiraled down and circled around the monster's claws as it gathered its power.

Harley looked left and right, but there was nothing else in sight, no defense against the coming attack.

"Here," said Kenyon Moor as he stepped up beside Harley. "Let's try this." He held up his hand, and Harley saw that Kenyon was holding the odd, black tube he had fired at the elevator door. Kenyon reached into the pocket of his jeans, came out with a small cylinder of dull metal, and shoved it into the end of the tube.

As Kenyon raised his weapon, Harley was surprised by the expression on his face. There was no anger, no rage—only calm determination.

The Billie-thing glared down at them and screeched.

"Payback time," said Kenyon. He pressed the buttons on the black tube.

There was a solid thump, and the air in front of the weapon twisted and bulged. The squirming knot of madness swarmed across the room and struck the floating creature.

The shot blasted Billie away like a baseball flying off a bat. It struck the window at the end of the room, shattering it into a million glittering fragments. The broken glass slid away toward the street far below.

A sharp breeze whistled through the jagged opening and cut across the forest. The crimson light of the setting sun streamed in.

The force of the strange gun had flayed the monster alive. It hung in the air in front of the shattered window with bare, writhing muscles exposed and scaly skin hanging down its torn flaps. The long snout was shattered and split. Curved teeth fell along with a shower of black gore. The wounded beast scrambled at the edge of the broken pane with clawed hands and clawed feet as it struggled to stay away from the drop beyond.

"Kill you," it croaked. Its voice was wet and choked, but still filled with a terrible fury. "Kill you all." Slowly, it began to climb back into the room.

"Shoot it again!" Harley shouted.

Kenyon only shook his head and tossed the weapon to the ground. "No more ammo," he said.

The thing in the window gave a wet, inhuman laugh.

A hand reached up from the floor and grabbed the creature by its scaly ankle. Agent Cain stood and shoved the thing that had masqueraded so long as a human being. The creature tore at him, ripping the skin of his face and shredding his clothes, but Cain did not let go. He forced the monster through the opening and out into the chill air.

For a moment, it seemed that the creature would

continue to hover, like some cartoon character who had not yet noticed that its feet had left the earth. Then it began to drop, screaming toward the ground. As it passed, the clawed hands made one last swipe, snagging the torn, burned coat of Agent Cain.

With a grunt of surprise, Cain was jerked from his feet and pulled through the opening.

"No!" shouted Harley. She ran toward the broken window.

Cain clung to a lip of granite so thin it was smaller than the space of his fingertips. Behind him, the reptilian creature was climbing upward, its claws digging into the agent's legs as it pulled its way toward the opening.

Harley reached out. "Take my hand," she said.

The agent shook his head. "If you . . . pull me in," he gasped. "You let . . . her in as well."

The Billie-thing gave another hissing laugh. It swung its arms higher, and its claws sank into Cain's back. The agent's face stretched tight with agony.

"We'll stop her," said Harley. "Just take my hand."

"No," said Cain. He winced again as the creature on his back tore at his flesh. "I said . . . it was about time . . . for me to retire. It seems . . . I was right."

Cain released his grip on the wall.

The Billie-thing screamed wildly and scrambled for the opening, but it was too late. Together Cain and Billie plummeted toward the street more than four hundred feet below.

Harley stood at the edge of the forest and watched the jaguar.

She had noticed the big cat following her soon after Cain and Billie had died, and it had not been far from Harley since. At first, she had been afraid of the beast. She wondered if the cat intended to take revenge on the people who had killed its master. But the longer Harley stared into the jaguar's yellow eyes, the more certain she became that the cat would not attack. More than anything, the animal seemed confused.

Harley wondered if Billie had controlled the jaguar's mind the way she had controlled Kenyon's—filling the animal with thoughts of rage and murder. It had certainly seemed like a killer when it had cornered them by the elevator door. Now it seemed more pitiful than scary.

"You'll be all right," Harley whispered to the cat. "Someone will show up soon. They'll probably take you to a nice zoo."

The jaguar stared back, unblinking.

"Harley!" called a distant voice.

Harley turned and waved her hands. "Over here!" she shouted back.

With the sun down, the rooftop forest was full of

darkness and shadows. If there was a light switch in the place, no one had been able to find it.

Kenyon Moor emerged from the shadows. "We got the elevator fixed," he said. "We should go. I mean, if you're ready." Kenyon looked away into the darkness.

Harley's lips curled up in a smile. Kenyon still felt a terrible sense of embarrassment about the way Billie had manipulated him. His normal arrogance and certainty had taken a big dent. Harley didn't expect it to last. Kenyon was far too stubborn to let anything keep him down for long. "I'm ready," she said. "Let's get moving."

"Right," Kenyon nodded, but he didn't move. "Harley?"

"Yeah?"

"What Billie said about making herself look like you so I would want her—" He stopped and glanced up at Harley for a moment.

"Billie was controlling your mind," said Harley. "Besides, she would lie about anything to cause us more trouble."

Kenyon shook his head. "That part wasn't a lie. I do like you, Harley. More than that, I—"

Harley stepped forward quickly and pressed her fingers over his lips. "Not now," she said. "Not here. We've both been through too much. Once we're back in Stone Harbor, we'll talk."

A look of gratitude crossed Kenyon's face. He stepped back and nodded. "Right," he said. "I'll go find Dee and Scott, and we'll meet you at the elevator." He turned quickly and hurried off into the darkness.

For a few minutes, Harley stood in the shadows. She wasn't sure what she would say when she got back to Stone Harbor. Her feelings for Kenyon had been confused to begin with, and all the things that had happened over the last three days had not made sorting out her feelings any easier. She turned and looked back at the jaguar waiting under the trees. "You should be glad you don't have to make decisions like this," she told the cat. Then she turned back and started for the elevator.

She was crossing a field of high grass when she noticed a pale blue glow coming from the trees on her left. Curious, Harley turned away from the path and walked toward the light.

A screen of alder trees blocked her view for a moment. As she stepped between the trees, she was surprised to see a computer screen resting on the grassy earth at the center of a circular clearing.

Sitting cross-legged on the ground in front of the screen was Scott Handleson.

"What's this?" Harley asked.

Scott looked up. His face was pale in the glow of the screen, and the blue light cast a strange color over his blond hair, but there was a wide smile on his face. "This is wonderful," he replied.

Harley crouched down beside him and looked at

the stream of names and numbers flying past on the screen. "What is it?"

"This computer system seems to be tied into some kind of central database."

"Whose database?"

Scott shrugged. "I think it must be Umbra's."

"Umbra?" Harley looked again at the list of names. There were addresses on the screen, along with phone numbers and a string of numbers that meant nothing to her. "If this data really shows where all the Umbra members are, we need to make a copy. This could be just what we need to stop them once and for all."

Scott shook his head. "There's no disk drive on this thing, no printer, no storage of any kind that I can see. I've got no way to make a copy."

Harley frowned in frustration. Everything they needed to get an edge on Umbra was right here. "Use a pencil and paper, if you have to. We need to collect this information."

"Okay," Scott said. "In a second." He tapped ever faster on the keyboard, and more screens of data flashed.

"What are you looking for?" asked Harley.

Before he could answer, a shout rang across the forest. "Harley! Scott! Come quick! The police are on their way!"

Harley sighed. "We'd better move," she said. "Getting caught up here would probably mean we all spend the next ten years in prison."

"One second," said Scott, still hammering away.

The faint sound of approaching sirens drifted in through the broken window at the end of the long room. "Now," said Harley. She put her hand on Scott's shoulder. "Come on."

Dee Janes appeared through the screen of trees. "What are you two doing in here?" she asked. "Do you like the idea of going to Alcatraz?"

"Alcatraz is closed," Scott said without taking his eyes from the computer screen.

"Yeah, but for us I think they might open it up again." Dee turned to Harley. "I took a look at the policeman. He's still alive."

Harley smiled in relief. "That's good. I'm sorry he got tangled up in all this."

"You're going to be even sorrier if we don't get moving," said Dee. "From the looks of things out there, every cop in the city is on his way."

Suddenly Scott threw up his hands. "Yes!" he cried. "She's here!"

Harley frowned. "What are you talking about?"

Scott rammed his finger against the glass screen. "Chloe," he said. "The information about her is right here."

The sound of sirens grew closer, and Harley bit her lip. "Learn it quick."

"I've got it," said Scott. He stared at the screen a moment longer. "I won't forget." He jumped to his feet, spun around, and gathered Dee in a hug that lifted her from her feet. "I found her!"

"That's great," Dee said in a choked voice. "Let's talk about it when we're a thousand miles away, all right?"

Scott set her down, and together they hurried through the ring of trees.

For a moment, Harley stood alone in the clearing. She looked down at the computer screen. Billie might be gone, but there were hundreds of names on the scrolling screen, maybe thousands. Umbra was far from dead.

She turned and followed her friends into the darkness.

To be continued . . .

EVEN THE UNKNOWN WON'T STOP THEM

EXTREME ZONE #6

visit the website at http://www.simonsays.com
coming soon

Extreme Zone—where your nightmares become reality.... Kenyon and Harley were thrown together by circumstances beyond their control. Now they are bound together by forces beyond their comprehension. They must be careful whom they trust, for Kenyon and Harley have crossed the dark borders of the Extreme Zone, and anyone could lead them to certain doom—or to salvation.

**SEND IN TWO COMPLETED OFFICIAL ENTRY FORMS
AND RECEIVE A FREE
EXTREME ZONE BASEBALL CAP!**

Official Entry Form:

Name_____Birthdate_____

Address_____

City_____State_____Zip_____

Phone_____

An Archway Paperback
Published By Pocket Books

ARCHWAY PAPERBACKS

EXTREME ZONE #6

PROOF OF PURCHASE OFFER

OFFICIAL RULES

1. To receive your free EXTREME ZONE baseball cap (approximate retail value: $8.00), submit this completed Official Entry Form and at least one Official Entry Form from either books 1, 2, 3, 4 or 5 (no copies allowed). Offer good only while supplies last. Allow 6-8 weeks for delivery. Send entries to the Archway Paperbacks/EZ Promotion, 13th Floor, 1230 Avenue of the Americas, NY, NY 10020.

2. The offer is open to residents of the U.S. and Canada. Void where prohibited. Employees of Simon & Schuster, Inc., its parent, subsidiaries, suppliers, affiliates, agencies, participating retailers, and their families living in the same household are not eligible. One EXTREME ZONE baseball cap per person. Offer expires 12/31/97.

3. Not responsible for lost, late, postage due or misdirected responses. Requests not complying with all offer requirements will not be honored. Any fraudulent submission will be prosecuted to the fullest extent permitted by law.